ysteries:

out great
Hillerman

le . . . and
to a fresh,
snappy voice of crime fiction."   —*New York Newsday*

"The first mystery I've seen in which the truth is more frightening than fiction, the only mystery I have ever read in which I have felt that I might   victims."

"A delight for the gourmet of may   ters, a diabolically dovetailing plot   brittle writing this side of McBain. I   dawn on the tired horizon of the A

"Rivals even the best in the genre."   —

"A mystery lover's delight: clever   and chock full of detection lore. *M   much fun as finding a mint Christie   aunt's tea cosy."

                    —Carolyn Hart, author   an

"How ideal to play sleuth in the con   pealing and intriguing characters as N   Stevens—especially when their 'Dr.   eccentric hodge-podge of mystery fa   for an exciting new series."
                    —Joan Lowery Nixon, author of th   ies and past president of Myster

MORE MYSTERIES FROM THE
BERKLEY PUBLISHING GROUP ...

SISTER FREVISSE MYSTERIES: Medieval mystery in the tradition of Ellis Peters ...

by Margaret Frazer

PENNYFOOT HOTEL MYSTERIES: In Edwardian England, death takes a seaside holiday ...

by Kate Kingsbury

GLYNIS TRYON MYSTERIES: The highly acclaimed series set in the early days of the women's rights movement ... "Historically accurate and telling."—Sara Paretsky

by Miriam Grace Monfredo

MARK TWAIN MYSTERIES: "Adventurous ... Replete with genuine tall tales from the great man himself."—*Mostly Murder*

by Peter J. Heck

KAREN ROSE CERCONE: A stunning new historical mystery featuring Detective Milo Kachigan and social worker Helen Sorby ...

BY HOOK
OR BY BOOK

D. R. MEREDITH

BERKLEY PRIME CRIME, NEW YORK

BY HOOK OR BY BOOK

A Berkley Prime Crime Book / published by arrangement with the author

PRINTING HISTORY
Berkley Prime Crime mass-market edition / May 2000

All rights reserved.
Copyright © 2000 by Doris R. Meredith.
This book, or parts thereof, may not be reproduced
in any form without permission.
For information address: The Berkley Publishing Group,
a division of Penguin Putnam Inc.,
375 Hudson Street, New York, New York 10014.

The Penguin Putnam Inc. World Wide Web site address is
http://www.penguinputnam.com

ISBN: 0-425-17465-4

Berkley Prime Crime Books are published
by The Berkley Publishing Group,
a division of Penguin Putnam Inc.,
375 Hudson Street, New York, New York 10014.
The name BERKLEY PRIME CRIME and the BERKLEY PRIME CRIME
design are trademarks belonging to Penguin Putnam Inc.

PRINTED IN THE UNITED STATES OF AMERICA

10 9 8 7 6 5 4 3

To my husband, Mike Meredith,
felony prosecutor and string-figure enthusiast,
who first introduced me to Caroline Furness Jayne and
the possibility of a missing manuscript,
and who patiently created a simplified nomenclature
that a klutz like me could follow.
And thanks, too, to the International String Figure
Association, whose members were so helpful.

MEGAN CLARK'S
SIMPLIFIED NOMENCLATURE

String Length
Use a six-foot length of string and connect ends to make a loop.

Fingers and Hands
The fingers of each hand are numbered 1 to 5 beginning with the thumb. L stands for *Left*; R stands for *Right*; i.e., L1 = Left Thumb. H stands for *Hand*, and W stands for *Wrist*.

String and Loops
Loops are named after the finger they surround; i.e., Loop L1 = the loop around the left thumb. Each loop has a *near* string (*n*) and a *far* string (*f*). The near string is the string closest to finger

The far string is the string closest to finger 5.

Loops can be entered from *above* (the side nearest the fingertip); or *below* (the side nearest the knuckle).

When two loops surround a finger, the loop nearest the fingertip is the *upper* loop. The loop nearest the knuckle is the *lower* loop.

To *Navajo* a loop, lift the lower loop with the thumb and index of opposite hand, or with your teeth, up over the upper loop and over the finger or thumb.

To Pick Up, retrieve a string using the nail side of the finger; *To Hook Up,* retrieve a string using the fingerprint side of the finger, then straighten the finger by rotating it a half turn toward you or away, depending on the instructions.

To Hook Down, retrieve a string by using the fingerprint side of the finger, securing it in the crook of a bent finger. Frequently this finger remains with the fingertip touching the palm.

Perform all actions with both hands simultaneously. If an R or an L precedes a finger loop, or string name, perform the action on the indicated hand only.

OPENING A

All string figures mentioned in this account of the murderous events of August 7–10 begin with "Opening A."

1.   Assume the *Basic Position* in which hands are parallel with palms facing each other and fingers pointed up.

2.   Loop the string around both thumbs and stretch your hands until the loop is taut.

3.   *Pick up* the far thumb strings with your little fingers and stretch hands until string is taut. This is *Position One*.

4.   From *Position One,* using your right index finger (R2), *Pick Up* from below the string crossing

the left palm. Stretch hands until string is taut. Using your left index finger (L2) *Pick Up* string crossing right palm. Stretch hands until string is taut.

5. Congratulations! You have now completed "Opening A." Practice it several times until it becomes automatic, then turn the page and follow along.

PROLOGUE

Making string figures is a hobby familiar to every schoolchild who has ever played with a loop of string. More than a children's game, however, it is an art form common to virtually every culture in the world, from the Inuit of North America and Greenland to South Sea Islanders to American Indian tribes, from Europe to Asia to Africa to South America.

—MEGAN ELIZABETH CLARK,
"String Figures as Both Art and Culture."
Smithsonian, vol. 31, no. 4 (July 2000)

"Come in, come in."

The speaker swung open the door and stepped aside, bowing from the waist as he did so, a sarcastic gesture performed as it was by a person who confessed to being every bit as mercenary and unethical as a lawyer raiding his client's trust account. For all the visitor knew, the speaker was, in fact, such a lawyer.

"So you want another look at the manuscript? Didn't quite get off on your first touch? Oh, I've watched you people, salivating over a couple hundred pages of text and a few drawings like it was a copy of *Hustler.* You don't know what I'm talking about?

Never heard of that magazine? What century do you
people hang out in? Eighteenth? Nineteenth? Have
tea with Victoria, do you? You are a tight-assed
bunch . . . What? You don't care for that expression?
Is that what the pursed lips mean? You *disapprove*?
You look like you just bit into a raw persimmon. But
I guess you don't know much about persimmons, do
you, with your background. That's for us crude people of the lower socioeconomic classes in the Deep
South. Isn't that how you classify us? Lower socioeconomic classes? When you don't call us rednecks.
Because our daddies carried their lunches to work in
those black metal lunch boxes? If our daddies
worked. Maybe they laid around all day on the old
cast-off couch on the front porch, drinking beer and
telling dirty jokes. Is that what you think? What?
Why am I talking like this? Because none of you are
any better than me, with your talk of cultures and art
and contributing to the betterment of humankind.
You all want this manuscript. You all want to be a
part of publishing a Caroline Furness Jayne string-
figure book. You want to be the one who publishes
the famous lost manuscript of the Mother of String
Figures. You want to be *revered* by all the other nuts
who walk around with a loop of string in your shirt
pocket. Did I say loop of string? I meant several
loops of string. I've never met a string-figure enthusiast who only carried one loop. That's what gave me
the idea that these yellowed old pages with the faded
type and complicated directions might be worth
something. I bet you hate it that I was the one who

ran across that old trunk in a Pennsylvania antique store instead of you or any of the rest of the nuts at this convention. That includes the nuts in that reading group. Hey, maybe I can find a lost Agatha Christie or Dorothy Sayers. Or maybe not. Those two old gals were businesswomen par excellence. Had all their manuscripts locked up in safety-deposit boxes with the names of their heirs on each one. Those two English ladies used their heads for something besides hanging those silly-looking hats on. What is it about English and hats? Must be something genetic. You know what I ought to do instead? I ought to go down under and search for an Arthur Upfield manuscript. Nobody made much of a fuss over him when he was alive, but I'll bet you the Jayne manuscript against a million dollars that an unknown Upfield manuscript would set up my retirement fund in good shape.

"A million dollars? You think that bet is my way of telling you what the Caroline Furness Jayne manuscript is worth? I don't think so. If a million dollars is what your sealed bid amounts to, then you've lost this silent auction. Or did you come back to change your bid?

"No? You don't want to change your bid? You just want to study the manuscript a little more? I don't know that I can let you do that. The rules I announced this morning specified that each person who wished to make a bid had fifteen minutes to study, read, touch, fantasize about, or whatever they wanted to do, save copy any part of the manuscript. I do have some principles whether you believe it or not, and I don't think I'll break my own rules. You may submit an additional bid if you wish—I didn't specify how many bids an individual might make—but you may not touch the manuscript. You're all such experts about Caroline Furness Jayne that surely you could spot a forgery in the blink of an eye, so to speak. Not that this is, however much you wished it was. That's what's got you all so hot and bothered—if you cold-blooded academic types could get hot—the manuscript is the real thing.

"I know why all of you are desperate to have a look. I'm aware that Caroline Furness Jayne was so worshiped by her family that information about her is difficult to find. That the Furness family, old Philadelphia Main Line to a man or a woman, and Jayne, her husband—no slouch himself as far as money was concerned—simply grieved themselves nearly to death and hardly ever spoke to the press about her. That while you all can quote from her first book at great length—that's no lie, she's been quoted more than the Bible at a Baptist church on Sunday morning—none of you know a great deal about her private life. Not any more than was disclosed in the biographical sketch by Mike Meredith that appeared in your bulletin. Ain't that a shame. Where is the *National Enquirer* when you need it.

"I'm a Philistine, am I? I have no appreciation of the significance of string-figure art? That it is symbolic of cultural beliefs, that it is folk art? Oh, I recognize the art of a complex string figure as well as the next man.

"I don't? The average person feels a primeval identification with string figures that I obviously do not feel? That if a person seated in a crowded airport pulled a loop of string out of his pocket and began constructing string figures, he would soon be surrounded by people of all creeds and colors, all talking about string figures they remember from their childhoods? So you think I wouldn't be a member of any such crowd? You're probably right. I'm not much for rubbing elbows with my fellowman. As for my fellow woman, I prefer rubbing softer areas than elbows.

"Oh, that offended you, did it? I seem to be doing a lot of that lately. But I predict all of you will overlook my offensive behavior—or should I say politically incorrect?—because I own the Jayne manuscript and you don't. And you all want it."

The speaker turned and walked to the desk the motel furnished each room, a rather elegant piece of furniture stained a dark cherry and reminiscent of an age when elegant ladies wore plumped hats in public and dashed off long letters to husbands or sweethearts or mothers or sisters or friends about activities while on holiday. The speaker lifted an unbound manuscript of yellowed pages and sat down in the chair behind the small desk. He looked up at his visitor, not at all intimidated that his seated position put him at a disadvantage in height. He had asked none of his visitors to sit, not that all obeyed the rules of good manners. That smartmouthed Megan Clark merely smiled and sat down in the Windsor chair in the cor-

ner of the motel room as if he had invited her to be
seated. He despised Generation X'ers for their self-
proclaimed independence of his generation's rules.
Not that he should be bothered by Megan Clark,
however she behaved. She was penniless, and only
came to look at the manuscript. She couldn't afford
to buy it if he sold it for the price of a T-bone steak.

The speaker saw the visitor walk behind the chair,
and quickly slipped the manuscript into the shallow
center drawer of the desk. "No fair reading over my
shoulder. Or did you want to make a string figure
following Caroline Furness Jayne's directions, maybe
one of the Nauru Island figures, just for the fun of it
in case you lose tomorrow's silent auction? Oh, so
you're going to demonstrate for me, eh? Okay, I'll
play along. Wait! What are you doing? No! No!"

Whether the speaker planned to trade the manuscript for his life, or what his last words might have
been had the strong nylon string held by hands made
powerful and flexible by years of making string figures not choked him into unconsciousness in twenty
seconds, is a matter of conjecture. Within forty seconds his brain was dead, starved of the blood sugar
more essential for its existence than oxygen, and beyond any thoughts whatsoever. His body lived another three and one half minutes. By the time he was
dead, the visitor was gone after arranging a particularly suitable string figure whose irony the visitor's
fellow enthusiasts would appreciate.

1

CAT'S CRADLE

A game of string figures found in China, Korea, Japan, the Philippines, and Borneo, as well as Austria, Germany, the Netherlands, Denmark, Sweden, Switzerland, France, and England. In southern China it is called *Kang sok,* meaning "Well Rope"; in Germany, one of its various names is *Hexenspiel,* or "Witch's Game."

1. Loop the string around the back of the fingers, leaving the thumb free.

2. R1 and R2 (Right Thumb and Right Index Finger) pick up near string on left hand and wrap it counterclockwise around the left hand, once again leaving thumb free. Stretch string taut.

3. L1 and L2 (Left Thumb and Left Index Finger) pick up near string on right hand and wrap it counterclockwise around the right hand, leaving thumb free. Stretch string taut.

4. Finish Opening A, using first R3 and then L3 (Right and Left Middle Fingers) to pick up from below the string across the palm. Stretch string taut. You have constructed the cradle, the first

of many variations of the game. The other variations require two players, and begin with the cradle.

"Ryan! Pick up the near string with R1 and R2! That means retrieve the string nearest you with your right thumb and right index finger, then loop it around all four fingers on your left hand. No! No! Counterclockwise! It's really very simple if you would only concentrate."

Ryan Stevens, professor of history at West Texas A&M University and curator of historical collections at the Panhandle-Plains Museum on the same campus, looked down with a bewildered expression at the tangled loop of string on his hands. "I am concentrating, Megan, but I think that just makes it worse. Maybe if you show me a picture of how the string figure is supposed to look when it's finished, the directions would make more sense."

Megan Clark tapped her foot in its Doc Marten sandal as she sat on the porch of Ryan's bungalow and silently counted to ten. How fortunate for the children of Texas that she had resisted her mother's advice and avoided all education classes at the University of Texas at Austin, because she apparently had absolutely no gift for teaching. Or else Ryan had no gift for learning. But he was a brilliant historian. His classes on the Western Movement had waiting lists of students eager to attend, and his lectures on Custer and the Battle of the Little Big Horn always drew standing-room-only crowds. He knew the his-

tory of every block of Amarillo, and anywhere else
you could think of in the Texas Panhandle, along
with the rest of the West, but when it came to constructing string figures, he was a klutz. It puzzled her
how he could braid leather into all kinds of intricate
objects, but couldn't make a Cat's Cradle to save his
life. Every school-age child could make a Cat's Cradle, even children on Pacific islands with no written
language.

"Uh, Megan. I can't get this string off my fingers.
I think I made a couple of knots again. Whatever I
did, I'm losing circulation in my thumb and index
finger on my right hand."

Megan again counted to ten, drew a deep breath,
and smiled in what she hoped was a kindly manner.
Ryan was her best friend, but sometimes he was not
only helpless, but hopeless. She wondered how he
had managed to care for himself during his one-year-
plus of being a widower.

"Don't pull the string any tighter, Ryan. Put your
palms together so the string loosens up a little."

"I can't seem to get my palms any closer without
dislocating my little finger. Excuse me, I meant L5."

Megan pulled her Swiss Army knife out of her
pocket and opened it to the smallest blade. "Hold
still, and I'll cut the string off you."

He held up his hands, now so entangled in string
that Megan didn't know where to cut first. "You know,
Ryan, I've led you through every step, watched you
with every bit of my concentration, and I can't figure
out how you end up with such a snarl. I didn't know

that a six-foot loop of string could even make such a mess."

"I didn't either. I must have wound the string clockwise instead of counterclockwise. Or maybe I picked up when I should have hooked down." He grinned at her, his eyes crinkling at the corners.

Ryan Stevens was the only person Megan knew with eyes so blue and vivid that they looked like neon light. Add wavy black hair with just a little silver at the temples, broad shoulders, and slim hips, and he was a handsome man even if he was in his forties. Fortunately, he didn't know he was handsome. In her opinion, nobody was more obnoxious than a handsome man who knew it. Give her the ugly ones anytime. They try harder to please.

Megan cut the loop in two places, unwound it from Ryan's fingers, and gathered up the pieces. "Flex your fingers until circulation is restored, Ryan. I would hate to be responsible for your getting blood poison."

"I'm sorry, Megan. I guess my coordination is not as good as I thought."

Megan drew another deep breath and blew it out. "Never mind, Ryan. I guess certain people just don't have the kind of eye-hand coordination necessary for making string figures. It's not your fault. You were born that way. But it would have been helpful if you could have followed my nomenclature so I would know if the average person could re-create my directions. Sometimes editors are picky. If they can't duplicate an example, they presume no one can. That's not necessarily the case most of the time, but I can't get into an argument with the editors either. These are the people who control my destiny. I *have* to write articles for the professional journals, the kind with a circulation of five hundred or less, so I don't completely drop out of sight. I mean, if I ever want a job on a dig as an archaeologist or anthropologist, not to mention a paleopathology position, I have to keep up my credentials some way or the other. I thought this article on string figures was a natural. I thought I might even be able to sell it to the *Smithsonian*. Imagine that, Ryan, my selling an article to a magazine that paid me in real money instead of copies of the publication."

"You deserve it, Megan. No one could have worked harder than you. Why, you've been sharing your knowledge of string figures with me every night for six weeks."

Ryan's expression was sincerity itself, but Megan caught a certain inflection in his voice that made her wonder if he was being entirely truthful. She decided he was. Not only was Ryan too intrinsically honest to lie well, but he stuttered when he tried. "I'm so glad I have a friend who will listen to me while I brainstorm an article. You have no idea how helpful it is to have an audience off whom I can bounce ideas."

"I've been meaning to speak to you about that," Ryan began.

"String figures reveal so much anthropological information that we might not know any other way,"

Megan continued, beginning to pace up and down Ryan's porch, gesturing with her hands the way she always did when she had, as her mother put it, "the bit between her teeth." "Think of them as abstract illustrations of a people's deepest and most sincere responses to, for example, the effects of weather on the environment. The Navajo have string figures representing lightning and storm clouds. That's pretty important stuff if you live in an environment with hardly any rainfall as the Navajo do."

"I'm familiar with weather on the Navajo reservation."

"Of course you are, Ryan. You're an expert on Western history, and that includes the Southwestern Indian tribes."

"I have several close friends who live on the reservation."

"Then I'm not surprised you're so interested in string figures. It's part of your friends' culture that you can share. String figures can be three-dimensional symbols of religious beliefs, or representations of a culture's justice system or even of animals and birds. Young children who can't read or write, who live in the depths of jungles or the far reaches of the Arctic, who have never even seen a television set, can create the most elaborate string figures—some with eight or ten variations. It's phenomenal."

Ryan nodded his head, an earnest expression on his face, and Megan smiled and softened her voice. "But you, with three advanced degrees from very good universities, can't even make a Cat's Cradle. I don't understand."

Ryan shrugged as he rubbed his hands together to restore circulation. "It's a puzzle to me, too. I just don't have the knack for it, I guess, but I hate to see you waste all that information. Maybe you should share your enthusiasm with the rest of the members of the Murder by the Yard Reading Circle. They're a curious bunch."

Megan wasn't sure just what exactly Ryan meant by the term "curious bunch," but she decided to take his advice anyway.

Two weeks later she was glad she had, because all the members of the Murder by the Yard Reading Circle went bonkers over string figures. Agnes Caldwell, the proprietor of the Time and Again Bookstore where Murder by the Yard held its weekly meetings, ordered copies of *String Figures and How to Make Them: A Study of Cat's Cradle in Many Lands* by Caroline Furness Jayne for each member of the group.

"Thank goodness the book is still in print," Agnes said as she passed out copies of what Megan privately called "the Bible of String Figures," a trade-size paperback with three intricate string figures drawn in white on the cover. "Otherwise I would have had to scour the used-book market for copies."

"I don't think you would have had much luck, Agnes," said Megan. "You might say *String Figures and How to Make Them* is a book of limited interest."

"Oh, I don't think that's entirely true, Megan," said

Rosemary Pittman, an elderly lady with a head of bouncy curls obviously coiffed by a talented hairdresser. "I tried some of the variations on the Apache Door while I was under the hair dryer at the beauty shop this morning, and before I could turn around, almost everyone in the shop was watching, and several asked where they could learn how to do string figures. Naturally, I told them to come to Time and Again Bookstore on Sixth Street, Agnes, so you may be ordering a lot more of Mrs. Jayne's book."

"And I demonstrated the Zulu string figure called the Moth," said another white-haired lady, who looked nearly identical to Rosemary Pittman, except her hair was the result of a home permanent, skillfully done, but a home permanent all the same, as any woman in the group would recognize. "I did it at my ladies' missionary society meeting. We were discussing our budget for Africa, and it seemed appropriate. Everyone was fascinated, so I suggested we do string figures from each country where we sponsor a missionary. Well, you know us Baptists. We take missionary work very seriously, and we sponsor missionaries to nearly every country in the world. So I suspect you will need to order lots more of Mrs. Jayne's book than just for the ladies at Rosemary's beauty shop."

Lorene Getz sat back and smiled at Agnes and Megan, obviously proud that she had spread the word about string figures in addition to spreading the word.

Rosemary clapped her hands, as did Agnes and the

other members of the group. "Lorene, I'm so proud of you. That's such a wonderful idea that I'll mention it at my ladies' missionary society meeting, too. You know, we Methodists are also well known for our missionary efforts."

The two ladies smiled and nodded at each other, and Megan knew that every member of both missionary societies would dutifully come to Time and Again Bookstore and buy copies of Jayne's books, not necessarily because every lady was dying to learn how to make string figures, but because Rosemary and Lorene suggested they do so. In the Deep South, influential women like Rosemary and Lorene were referred to as "steel magnolias." Megan thought that a good name to call such ladies in the Texas Panhandle would be "steel mesquites." Even the botany department at Texas A&M found the mesquite tree to be ineradicable, so Megan figured the missionary societies didn't have a prayer of withstanding Rosemary and Lorene.

Herbert—"Call Me Herb"—Jackson III cleared his throat. "I did a demonstration at my bar association meeting this month, and was gratified at how many of the members stayed awake."

Megan smiled at Call Me Herb. He had rushed to defend her last spring when Lieutenant Jerry Carr of the Potter-Randall-Armstrong Special Crimes Unit had suspected her of murdering an unpleasant member of the reading group. She was innocent, of course; otherwise, she wouldn't be sitting here on Agnes's comfortable couch in the reading area of the

Time and Again Bookstore. But she had appreciated
Herb's ability as a criminal defense attorney, even
though she suspected he was as successful as he was
because he was so boringly honest himself that no
jury believed he would defend anyone guilty of more
than running a red light. Not that her case ever made
it as far as the courtroom. She, with the help of Ryan
and the other members of Murder by the Yard, had
trapped the real murderer and recorded a confession.
Jerry Carr, of course, lectured her on interfering with
an investigation, etc., but Megan forgave him. After
all, no man likes to be shown up by a young woman
who stands five feet two inches only if she wears
heels or shoes with very thick soles, has curly red
hair, and is described by every person who sees her
as "cute."

Dr. Megan Elizabeth Clark, Ph.D. in physical anthropology with a specialty in paleopathology, hated
the word "cute." Some days she thought she might
actually be tempted to commit physical violence on
the next person to use the C-word. Surely there were
other words more suitable—freckle-faced came to
mind, although Ryan denied she had enough freckles
to earn that descriptive tag.

Herb had never—to her knowledge, at least—described her as "cute." For that, he gained her loyalty
and friendship.

The last time Herb mentioned giving a program at
his bar association meeting was the unfortunate oc-
casion that he chose to read a chapter of his work in
progress, a legal thriller which even Agnes admitted

put her to sleep after reading three paragraphs. During the reading, one of the district judges fell asleep, tipped forward in his chair, and landed facedown in a dish of chocolate mousse the waiter had quietly set on the table in front of him. Unfortunately, the judge inhaled a noseful of the dessert before he woke up, and suffered the indignity of having CPR performed on him by a female member of the bar whom the judge had once described as having "a face that looked like five miles of bad road." The judge's wife told her bridge club that her husband had purple bruises on his chest for weeks after the lifesaving procedure. When the paramedics loaded him on the stretcher to carry him to the ambulance, the female bar member described to them what had happened. Apparently she was a better storyteller than Call Me Herb, because the paramedics broke into hysterical laughter, dropped the stretcher and the judge, who rolled down the six marble steps in the front of the country club and broke his arm.

Ever since that day, according to the gossip Megan heard, Herb and the female bar member refused any case that might be tried in the judge's court, fearing that the judge, not known to be charitable toward attorneys who, as the saying goes, "got on his bad side," might be less than unbiased toward their clients.

"Herb, that's terrific," said Megan. "You must have really held their attention."

Herb nodded, looking somewhat bewildered by his success. "Several of them asked me about taking lessons, but I recommended they buy Ms. Jayne's book instead."

Megan doubted that Caroline Furness Jayne, who died a premature death of typhoid in 1909, would have appreciated being labeled a "Ms." Marriage was taken a lot more seriously at the turn of the century than it seemed to be now.

"Well, if everyone is going to regale us with tales of their efforts to popularize string figures, I suppose I ought to share my efforts with the group," declared Dr. Randal Anderson, a professor of English at Amarillo College. He stroked his goatee, a rather sparse growth of facial hair that he now at least kept neatly trimmed, more at the behest of Candi Hobbs, the current object of his romantic attentions and also a member of Murder by the Yard, than because of any inherent impulses toward neatness. In his pre-Candi days, the beard had had the appearance of an overgrown patch of lawn with occasional bare spots.

"I shared some of my knowledge of string figures with my English classes. We were studying Chaucer, so I demonstrated the Saw and the Parachute, which turns into the Bunch of Keys."

"But those string figures were collected from Scotland," said Megan. "Chaucer was not from Scotland."

"Well, if you're going to get technical about it," retorted Randal, rubbing his goatee instead of stroking it, a mannerism Megan noticed whenever the English professor was peeved.

"We couldn't find any string figures that originated in England," said Candi, blinking her eyes. She had recently exchanged her thick glasses for contact lenses and was not making a good adjustment. A graduate student at West Texas A&M University, Candi was writing her master's thesis on mystery fiction, which explained both her membership in Murder by the Yard and her propensity to talking in footnotes about any particular selection the group discussed. Megan never saw the purpose of knowing the South African publication dates of Agatha Christie's novels.

"That's because there aren't any. Cat's Cradle, which is first mentioned in English literature in 1768, is not indigenous to England, although most people think so. It actually was introduced in the seventeenth and eighteenth centuries when the tea trade with China began," said Megan.

"Well, my students weren't so worried about the technicalities. They enjoyed the string figures anyway. And I referred them to Time and Again Bookstore, Agnes, so you may have a gaggle of students wanting Jayne's book."

"Thank you, Randal. Thank all of you. Gracious, I might make a noticeable enough profit on these string-figure books alone. But don't you think it's time we moved on to tonight's mystery selection?" suggested Agnes. "Sue Grafton is one of my favorite authors, and I'm glad Megan suggested we start our discussion of her work by reading her very first book. 'A' Is for Alibi started an epidemic of female-private-eye heroines of mystery series. There hadn't been many before Grafton wrote Kinsey Millhone."

"Could I ask one question first?" asked Randal.

"He's never asked just one question in his life," Ryan whispered in Megan's ear. "And Grafton didn't write *to* Kinsey Millhone; she wrote *about* her. Do you think Agnes's brain is still skipping a little every now and then since she was attacked by the murderer last year? It takes a while to recover from a brain injury."

"What is it, Randal?" asked Megan, patting Ryan's arm but otherwise ignoring him. Ryan Stevens's total experience with mysteries before joining Murder by the Yard was reading Poe and Conan Doyle in college and watching three Agatha Christie movies. She wasn't sure his repertoire of mysteries had increased any, although he did have Grafton's main character's name right. Ryan really ought to stay awake more during reading-circle discussions.

"I would just like the group's opinion on whether the length and thickness of the loop of string should be included in the directions for the figure. Sometimes I have a devil of a time making a figure only using a six-foot loop."

"I think that's a legitimate question, Megan," said Lorene. "Sometimes I think I need a longer string."

Megan sat up a little straighter on the couch and cleared her throat. "Before we argue about that, I have an announcement to make. I wrote to the International String Figure Association inviting them to Amarillo in August for a string-figure convention. I thought that since all of you were enjoying constructing string figures so much, you might enjoy helping me with the convention."

There was silence for a moment, then everyone talked at once.

"You mean, the string-figure association accepted?"

"The ISFA is coming to Amarillo?"

"You want us to help organize the convention?"

Megan clapped her hands for silence. "The answer to all your questions is yes. I have a list here of duties for which I would like each of you to take responsibility. Since Ryan has had more experience with conventions than the rest of us, I've assigned him the responsibility of organizing the workshops." She didn't think the group needed to know that Ryan's experience with conventions was limited to attending the Western Writers of America Conference each June.

2

M y name is Ryan Stevens, curator of history at the Panhandle-Plains Museum on the campus of West Texas A&M University in Canyon, Texas, some twelve miles from the Time and Again Bookstore on Sixth Street, and maybe fifteen from the High Plains Motel, where the event some of the more sarcastic members of Murder by the Yard insist on calling "The Convention of Murder" took place. Actually, Dr. Randal Anderson is the only member who calls the meeting of string-figure enthusiasts late last summer by such a lurid name, but then Randal considers himself to be witty. I disagree.

I am also a professor of American history, and teach two courses at the university: Manifest Destiny and Westward Expansion in the Nineteenth Century, and Frontier Life in the American West, plus several seminars on the Battle of the Little Big Horn. That's the Custer massacre for those of you unfamiliar with the West. I mention these facts because it explains my love of the Western, those novels our parents—

or at least, my father—called shoot-'em-ups. That is a narrow definition for a genre that also includes such novels as *The Big Sky* by A. B. Guthrie, *The Travels of Jaimie McPheeters* by Robert Lewis Taylor, *Shane* by Jack Schaefer, *The Day the Cowboys Quit* and *The Good Old Boys* by Elmer Kelton, *Hondo*, and my personal favorite by Louis L'Amour, *Conagher*. Only a man with a name like L'Amour could have written a Western love story like *Conagher*. If you've never read it, you ought to. Sam Elliott made a fine movie out of it, too. Megan Clark calls it a chick flick, because she always cries when the woman named Edie (played by Katharine Ross) ties letters onto tumbleweeds in the hope that someone will answer her. Megan says that is the loneliest act a woman could perform. Being a woman, I suppose she would know, at least theoretically. Megan has always been one who enjoyed her own company, so I can't imagine her lonely. But then she attracts people like a magnet attracts metal filings, so I suppose she has had few chances to actually be lonely.

There are lots of other wonderful Westerns: *Lonesome Dove* by Larry McMurtry, just about any title by Richard S. Wheeler, although my favorite is *Comstock*, and a beautifully written little novel called *Aces and Eights* by Loren Estleman, who is also a fine mystery writer, Megan tells me.

I wouldn't know. I don't read many mysteries. Actually, I've read only one since I joined the Murder by the Yard Reading Circle: *"A" Is for Alibi,* and we never did get around to discussing it. I thought it was well written, but I never knew a woman who would live in a converted garage. Except maybe Megan. My late wife would have seen mice and cockroaches in every corner and never set foot in it. Megan spent a year as a student resident assistant at the University of Texas Natural History Collection, so not much that crawls, scurries, or slithers bothers her.

Those of you who know nothing of the events of last spring may be wondering what I'm doing in a mystery reading club if I don't read mysteries. It's simple. Megan Clark.

Megan Clark has lived next door to me all her life—except those years she spent earning three degrees in archaeology and physical anthropology. She was my oldest daughter Evin's best friend, and was always underfoot when she was growing up. I always noticed her. I couldn't help it. She was a thin little girl with the reddest, curliest hair in Amarillo, a peaches-and-cream complexion when every other girl her age was hiding "zits" under Band-Aids, a few freckles across her nose, and one limb or the other in a cast. As I remember, Megan broke both arms and both legs at least once, and I recall seeing one arm in a cast two summers in a row. Her mother told my wife that she was afraid to take Megan back to the emergency room again because the nurses and doctors suspected her of child abuse. Fortunately, Megan grew out of her propensity to break bones at about that time, so all turned out well.

Megan still lives next door to me on Ong in Amarillo, Texas, and she still lives with her mother, not because she can't cut the apron strings—Megan's mother isn't the type to wear aprons, real or theoretical—but because she doesn't have to pay rent, so she can save practically her whole salary as an assistant reference librarian. To explain to those who are unaware of Megan's work history, yes, she is a Ph.D. in physical anthropology with a specialty in paleopathology, but that means she autopsies mummies, and there aren't many mummies requiring an autopsy in the Texas Panhandle—or anywhere else for that matter. When there is, every archaeologist and anthropologist with any experience in such fields as old bones, old seeds, old fibers, and old guts is immediately volunteering for the privilege of suiting up to delicately examine the dissected insides. A recent Ph.D. at twenty-six, Megan is somewhere at the bottom of the employment list, so she works as a librarian and saves her money in case as a last resort, she has to fund her own dig in search of an interesting mummy.

So what does all that have to do with my membership in a mystery reading group when I don't read mysteries, just because Megan signed me up?

Let me explain the circumstances. I am forty-five years old and have been a widower for nearly two years. Once I worked through my grief, I discovered that I missed sex. I know certain of you are laughing, because even as I write these words, I am surprised. I *was* surprised. My wife and I had married young and I was faithful to her, so sex had been like the evening meal: it was always on the table. I won't bore you with my several embarrassing attempts at dating, including single clubs at churches, one humiliating evening at a singles bar where I kept running into my students, and an off-and-on relationship with an assistant professor of biology who turned out to know more biology than I did. Suffice it to say that when Megan returned to Amarillo, I embraced celibacy in return for friendship with a vibrant, brilliant young woman who really is cute, although I would cut out my tongue before I used that word in her presence.

But lately I've wondered if my thoughts about her are as pure as they ought to be. Whenever she mentions Lieutenant Jerry Carr—an ex-student of mine and head of the Special Crimes Unit—I experience what can only be described as a jealous fit. If complexions could turn green, mine would. Naturally, I don't mention these feelings to Megan. I'm old enough to be her father, for God's sake, although let me reassure everyone that she doesn't think of me as a fatherly figure. For one thing, I'm not familiar with the internal combustion engine, a prerequisite for anyone she might allow to replace the father who died when she was five. Megan fixes her own pickup, a black GMC behemoth with more miles on its odometer than I care to know. I refused to look anymore when it passed three hundred thousand. Megan is the only woman I know who not only owns her own toolbox, but knows the name of and how to use every tool in it.

She and Kinsey Millhone would probably be best friends.

But lust for a younger woman hardly explains my place in Megan's life.

I am not only her boon companion on whatever risky endeavor she undertakes, such as rock climbing, but I am her Watson. When she insisted on playing female sleuth last spring, I recorded our "case," based on notes and observations I had made and Megan's brief jottings in a notebook the size of a pack of cigarettes. One day I may be a literary giant in the mystery field because I was Megan Clark's Watson.

Why Watson? As the older member of our duo, as the professional historian and curator used to tedious detail, why wasn't I the Holmes figure?

Simple. I don't do blood, and I don't do seeping fluids from fresh corpses. Neither bothers Megan enough to notice. Also, Megan is an archaeologist and anthropologist, which anywhere but the United States, makes her a scientist, and one who can take a body *in situ* and make it confess to its last few minutes of life better than any pathologist or medical examiner I ever heard of. She sees a thousand details, finds the one which doesn't fit the scenario of death, and traces it back to the perpetrator. I don't notice the details until they are written up on a piece of paper because I'm too busy either fainting or vomiting. I have a reputation of sorts among the paramedics in town because of the number of times I required reviving from a faint after Megan and I discovered a fresh corpse last spring. Each time I revived, I remembered the copious amounts of blood and fainted again. One paramedic suggested therapy, but I believe he was once a student of mine who failed one of my courses.

At any rate, my sensibilities settle the pecking order in our duo of amateur sleuths. Megan is Holmes and I'm Watson.

There is another reason for Megan's ascendency in our relationship. She studies the artifacts remaining from human activities, whether a mummy or a sandal still on the foot of a man who froze to death in the Alps two thousand years ago. Of course, she probably would be more interested in the mummy than in the sandal, but that's beside the point. Megan studies humans in their daily activities, makes connections between their possessions and their activities, and formulates theories to cover the reasons for their performing those particular activities in those particular ways—which, if you think about it, is another way of saying Megan studies motive, means, and opportunity—the same three questions one must answer in a murder investigation.

I, on the other hand, am more into the study of broad human events: heads of state, armies sweeping across plains, formally written treaties and alliances. Megan would be as much interested in what a particular head of state ate the morning he signed or refused to sign a treaty, or what chronic illnesses he suffered, as she would be in the terms of the treaty. I must confess that since becoming Megan's companion, I have paid more attention to the consequences on history of a leader's possible indigestion or gout. And toothaches. Have you ever considered how many bad historical decisions might have been made because a king or a general woke up one morning with a toothache? But I'm getting away from the subject, which is Megan's expertise in the areas most important to a murder investigation. The fact is she has it and I don't.

Besides, I've always had a secret ambition to write a book. I just never thought I would be writing a mystery instead of a Western.

But to get back to Megan and the Murder by the Yard Reading Circle . . . I was shocked into instant wakefulness by Megan's suggestion that I set up the workshops and seminars for some kind of convention she had persuaded the International String Figure Association to attend.

"I wouldn't want to take such a plum assignment away from any member of the reading circle, Megan," I said, hoping to start an argument over the subject of workshops and seminars that would get me off the hook so to speak. "Anyone here is more knowledgeable than I am. I'm the one who can't even make a Cat's Cradle. Remember?"

"You can't make a Cat's Cradle?" If a human can be said to hoot, then Randal hooted that sentence.

"I never claimed any dexterity at making string figures, Randal." I wish I had bitten my tongue rather than confess my total lack of ability at making a string figure, at least where Randal Anderson could hear me.

"Ryan has nearly as wide a knowledge of string-figure history as I do," said Megan with a steely-eyed look at Randal.

"That's right," I said. "I was Megan's only audience for a six-week-long lecture on string-figure history."

That sentence didn't come out exactly as I intended, but fortunately Megan didn't hear it, as having disposed of Randal's jeers at my clumsiness, she was too busy signing up volunteers for the convention.

I sighed and reached for her copy of *String Figures and How to Make Them* by Caroline Furness Jayne. I might as well get started on my part of the convention.

3

Every dog has his flea—if he is a normal dog.

—Deputy Police commissioner Parr
in Frederick Irving Anderson's
"The Recoil," *The Book of Murder*, 1930

Megan smoothed the wrinkles out of her convention T-shirt—plain white with a pair of hands demonstrating a string figure on the front, with *ISFA Convention, Amarillo, Texas, August 2001*, in black block letters on the back—patted her convention badge with its black-and-white ribbon with *Chairwoman* printed on it in capital letters, to make sure it was pinned on the left side of her shirt; checked to see that Rosemary and Lorene were seated beside her at the registration table; and took a deep breath. It was nearly ten o'clock—zero hour for opening registration, with the first official function of the convention a bare three hours away: an introductory luncheon where she would welcome string-figure enthusiasts from every state and several foreign countries.

She glanced about the lobby to make sure everything and, more importantly, everyone was in their place. There was Agnes manning the booth selling books and videos on string figures. An enthusiast from California who had the booth next to her was laying out exhibits of string in every possible color, length, and thickness, along with bags and boxes of various descriptions in which one might store string. Megan promised to buy herself a treat from that booth. Maybe some of the fluorescent-green-and-pink string, or the string holder that looked very much like a toolbox, at least on the outside.

At the end of the registration table sat Randal Anderson and his significant other, Candi Hobbs. Since Candi was so good at details, and Randal was always sure he was right, Megan had asked them to assist hotel personnel with assigning rooms to the registrants. Megan smiled at the dazed look on the hotel clerk's face as Candi greeted each registrant with a key and a registration card, as well as reciting a litany of needs each had specified needed filled. "Dr. Moser, you asked for a ground-floor room on the opposite side of the building from the swimming pool?"

"That's right, young lady. I enjoy watching young women in bathing suits as much as the next man, but at my age it's difficult to remember exactly why I enjoy watching them, so a room in a quiet area where I might possibly sleep undisturbed by squeals and splashes is a higher priority."

Candi blushed and blinked rapidly, and Megan wondered if she had caught the humor in the elderly gentleman's remark or just lost a contact lens under an eyelid. With Candi one never knew.

"I can't believe you're that old," said Candi, blink-

ing again. Megan felt her mouth drop open. Candi
flirting? With someone besides Randal? And she
wasn't blinking, she was batting her eyes. This was
nearly as astonishing as the discovery late last spring
during the reading circle's amateur sleuthing that
Randal Anderson had a sense of humor.

"I haven't had a pretty young woman tell me that
in at least thirty years," said the elderly gentleman.

Candi blushed and pushed her hair behind her left
ear without replying.

Rosemary leaned over and whispered in Megan's
ear. "He's probably the first man who ever told Candi
that she was pretty. That is just the sort of compliment his generation used to make to young women.
It might be a lie, but it was the kind that didn't hurt
anybody. Sometimes I miss those kinds of lies."

"You don't think Randal has told Candi that she's
pretty?" asked Megan.

Rosemary pursed her lips as she thought about the
question. "I don't think it would occur to Randal to
tell a kind lie. Not that he isn't very fond of Candi—I
think he is—but he's not a gentleman in the same
way that elderly man is."

"You requested a smoking room, Dr. Moser?"
asked Candi, frowning in disapproval. "You really
should try to quit smoking, you know. It's very bad
for your health."

Dr. Moser smiled, revealing a fine set of teeth that
Megan knew were original to him. If it was one thing
she knew, it was bones. "Young lady, I had a friend
nearly twenty years younger than I, which means he

must have been around seventy-five. He was in perfect health—no cholesterol, no prostate troubles, no arthritis, hadn't even lost his hearing. The man was the Charles Atlas of his age group. Of course, a young thing like you wouldn't know who Charles Atlas was. He was before your time. At any rate, my friend James was in perfect health until he stopped smoking. Within six months he was taking seventeen different prescription drugs for every conceivable ailment. Six months after that all his major organs shut down one after another. I was a pallbearer at his funeral last month. I swore then I'd never give up smoking my cigars. Much too risky."

"Oh, well, here's your key, and I'm sorry," said a befuddled Candi.

The gentleman smiled at Candi and leaned down to pinch her cheek. "Don't apologize, my dear. I'm not offended. Youth must have its crusades just as age must have its vices." He lifted his cane and pointed to the registration table. "I see I must pick up my registration packet over there where there are not one but three lovely ladies."

"Oh, here he comes, Megan, and he looks just like I always imagined Clark Gable would look if he had lived to be this gentleman's age," said Rosemary, sitting up straighter.

"Smile, ladies!" Herb Jackson III pointed a rather professional-looking camera in their direction. "Sir, if you would turn this way so I can get you in the picture, too."

"Ah, a mug shot," said Dr. Moser, turning toward the camera and leaning on his cane.

"No, it's for the *ISFA Bulletin* and the newsletter," said Herb.

Dr. Moser put his hand to one side of his mouth and whispered to Megan. "Methinks the gentleman lacks a sense of humor."

Megan grinned before she could stop herself. "He's an attorney. He can't help it."

"Ah, yes, a failing of the profession. But on to business. I am Dr. Solomon Moser, most probably the oldest living member of the International String Figure Association, and the only one to have actually met Caroline Furness Jayne."

"You're kidding!" Megan exclaimed. "You really met her! But she died in 1909!"

"My dear Miss"—he peered at her name tag—"Megan Clark. Dr. Clark, if I'm not mistaken."

"You're not. But how did you meet Caroline Furness Jayne?"

"I was born in 1905, Dr. Clark. I'll be ninety-six years young shortly. But to return to my story. I was a toddler and upper-crust Philadelphia society of the time looked down their noses at my mother for bringing a child to Sunday tea. It simply 'wasn't done.' Not that they snubbed my mother too heartily. My family had too much money to risk offending. But Caroline Jayne gave me toys and took me to the nursery where her two children were playing. Like every other male for whom she ever did a kindness, I fell

in love with Caroline Furness Jayne, and never met
a woman who was her equal."

The elderly man abruptly stopped speaking, drew
an immaculate white handkerchief from his pocket,
and dabbed at his eyes. He smiled at Megan. "I still
get a little emotional thinking about her. But to business. If you will be so kind as to give me my badge
and registration packet, I will walk across to the
workshops table where that rather frantic-looking
young man is trying to cope with all of us enthusiasts."

"That's Dr. Ryan Stevens. He's a historian," said
Megan.

"An honorable profession if not as well paying as
that of mathematician. Not that I ever made all that
much money in mathematics. I inherited my wealth
from a robber-baron father and had the good sense
to place it in the hands of a good stockbroker. Now,
that is a well-paying profession. Keep that in mind
when you marry, young lady."

"I will," said Megan, not seeing the need to tell
Dr. Moser that she had no intention of marrying until
she had uncovered and dissected at least one good
mummy. Actually, she wanted to discover an unknown Egyptian tomb, but she doubted there was one
left that hadn't been looted. The tomb of King Tut
was an exception.

"I have no doubt that you will. I have found that
women are more practical than men when playing the
game of love. Men tend to be romantics. That is why
we so often marry bad women. I did it twice myself.

The third time I married a 'good' woman. I was bored for thirty years." He lifted his cane and saluted the three woman. "I shall see you at the luncheon. Oh, is that Mark Sherman I see at the string exhibit? I must talk to him. Mark! Mark, hold up. I want to talk to you about a paper for the bulletin." Dr. Moser strolled across the lobby looking considerably younger than his ninety-five years.

"I'm nervous," Megan confessed as she tied her napkin into knots. "I know my face will turn red. It always does when I'm nervous."

"Don't expect me to sympathize with you," said Ryan. "You should have been sitting at my table, trying to convince those string-figure enthusiasts that I would not change the times of their workshops. What difference does it make anyway? I didn't schedule two workshops or seminars at the same time. In case you haven't noticed, Megan, some of these string-figure enthusiasts are teetering on the edge of obsessive-compulsive disorder. Have you met Denise LeClerc yet? She accused me of being a male chauvinist pig—God, I haven't heard that phrase since the seventies—for scheduling her workshop on string and how to use it after our trip to Dick Bivins Stadium to see the making of the Apache Door with five hundred feet of nylon rope by a Boy Scout troop. She even took exception to that. She wanted to know why we weren't using a troop of Girl Scouts. I'm not going to her workshop, by the way. There's no telling what kinds of uses for string she has in mind.

"I don't know why you let people bother you so much, Ryan. Just ignore their comments."

"Advice from someone who is so nervous about welcoming—what?—fifty string-figure enthusiasts that she's afraid her face will turn red," said Ryan, a glazed look in his eyes. "I'll tell you what I'm going to do. I'm going to hide out in the darkest corner of the bar this afternoon. I'd drink except I'm afraid you might get into trouble and need me, and I'm not much use when I'm drunk. My only solace in this whole affair is that at least it's cerebral, and completely harmless, so there will not be a repeat of last spring's unpleasantness. The United States might have a high murder rate, but a single, middle-class young woman cannot be expected to discover bodies more than once in a lifetime. Fresh bodies, that is, as opposed to mummies."

"Ryan, you're getting emotional. And you know you get sick after two drinks. Why don't you just eat your lunch while I welcome everyone? We'll all do these short self-introductions then adjourn for the afternoon's workshops. All you'll have to do is make sure that all the rooms have the proper signs in front of the doors."

Megan stood up and squared her shoulders, something she always did because she believed it made her look taller. Not much, but a little. "I'm not nervous anymore, Ryan. Isn't that remarkable?"

4

FISH SPEAR

According to Caroline Furness Jayne in her book *String Figures and How to Make Them,* this figure originates on Murray Island, Torres Straits, between Australia and New Guinea. It is called Pitching a Tent by the Silash Indians of British Columbia, and is also known to the Zuni Indians of New Mexico.

1. Position 1.

2. R2 (Right Index Finger) picks up the L Palmar (string across the left palm) string from above and turns finger toward you twice.

3. L2 (Left Index Finger) through the R2 (Right Index Finger) loop as in Opening A, and picks up the R Palmar (string across the right palm) string from below and extend.

4. Release R1 (Right Thumb) and R5 (Right Little Finger) and extend.

I'm emotional. I let comments bother me. Why don't I sit down and enjoy my lunch? All right. I can do that. My part is over. All I have to do the rest of the convention is to change the signs in front of the

workshop doors. I can manage that. If I can arrange
historical exhibits for the largest museum between
Dallas and Denver, I can change signs. This is, after
all, a calm, academic conference whose sole purpose
is for members and visitors to create string figures to
their heart's content. And if I practice the same calm,
academic self-control, I may make it through this
convention without strangling Megan Clark and the
rest of the Murder by the Book Reading Circle—who
ought to be home reading mysteries.

"What are you muttering about, Ryan?" asked Megan. "I'm having a hard time hearing the introduc-
tions over your monologue."

I folded my arms across my chest and shut up. I
certainly wouldn't want to be responsible for Megan
Clark missing an introduction—like the one the fellow in the corduroy suit was about to make. Corduroy in August in the Texas Panhandle?

"My name is Clyde Brownleigh, and I am about
to become the best friend of everyone in the room."

He stopped and smiled, not that a smile made him
any more attractive looking. I leaned over to whisper
to Megan. "There is some legend that I vaguely remember my grandmother telling me about, having to
do with the devil owning the souls of people with a
single long hairy caterpillar-looking eyebrow. She
would've taken one look at Clyde Brownleigh's eyebrow and said he was bad news. I guess he doesn't
own any tweezers."

"Ryan!"

She stabbed her elbow into my side, so I folded

my arms again. I didn't shut my mouth, however, because I needed it open while I tried to get my breath back. Megan doesn't kid around when she's irritated.

Brownleigh pushed back his corduroy coat and hooked his thumbs in his belt loops. I couldn't resist it. I leaned over to whisper in Megan's ear again. "I told you he was part devil. He isn't even sweating in that corduroy coat." I scooted my chair back so Megan's elbow missed me altogether.

"I am a collector of antiques—not in a large way, I haven't the money for that, but I do like looking around in antique stores for some little object or artifact that serious collectors may have overlooked. That's what I was doing in this grubby little store in Philadelphia, and not in one of the nicer areas of Philadelphia either. I was looking for something valuable that others had overlooked. And I found it! In a little tin trunk, buried under old sheet music from the turn of the century, was a manuscript."

He stopped and looked around at the people seated at the other tables, an expectant expression on his face. I suddenly started paying attention when I heard a low murmur from the other enthusiasts, and not just from a few, but from everyone. The only exceptions were the members of the Murder by the Yard Reading Circle, but only because they were new to the art of string figures.

Megan, however, wasn't. She grabbed my arm in a death grip. "Oh, my God, Ryan, he didn't! He couldn't! It's not possible."

I had no idea what she was talking about, but I found myself as much on the edge of my seat as anyone else in the room. Even the waiters who were picking up the luncheon plates and passing out the desserts were motionless.

Brownleigh smiled. "I found the lost Caroline Furness Jayne manuscript—her second book on string figures—in that grubby old antique store."

I had only learned about Caroline Furness Jayne and her *first* book six weeks ago, so I was totally bewildered by the mention of a lost manuscript, but I was the only one in the room who was.

Dr. Moser stood up, leaning on his cane. "Does it have the directions for making the Nauru Island figures?"

Brownleigh nodded. "Yes, it does. And it includes several Inuit figures that have been lost to history, and a multitude of Navaho and Apache figures as well as some from the pueblos of New Mexico."

"You will, of course, demonstrate the Nauru Island figures?" asked Dr. Moser.

"If our convention chairwoman and the program chairman would possibly make time available to me, I would be glad to demonstrate those figures and several others." Brownleigh cocked one side of that massive eyebrow at me.

Suddenly everyone in the room was crowded around the head table; specifically they were crowded around me, pulling at my T-shirt, tugging on my arms, and Dr. Moser, who I had thought was a civilized man, was poking his cane in my chest.

"Dr. Stevens, I believe I speak for everyone when I recommend that the schedule be altered to allow an entire day for Mr. Brownleigh's demonstrations. Personally, I will give up my workshop, and I'm certain others will, too." For an elderly man, Dr. Moser's voice was strong enough to be heard throughout the room.

I no longer had to worry about changing the signs for each workshop. Now I apparently had only one workshop, and that one didn't need a sign.

The High Plains Motel named all its conference rooms after local flora and fauna. There was a Mesquite Room, a Buffalo Room, a Palo Duro Canyon Room, a Yucca Room, and a Sagebrush Room. Clyde Brownleigh's demonstrations were scheduled for the Sagebrush Room, and every chair was taken long before two o'clock. Herb Jackson had a video camera set up to film the demonstrations, as well as a tape recorder on the podium to record every word Brownleigh uttered. Actually, Herb's efforts were superfluous, as nearly every enthusiast had his or her own video camera. Clyde Brownleigh would be the most filmed man in Texas today.

"Where is he?" asked Megan, wrinkling her forehead, a habit she had whenever she was worried.

I hugged her. I swear it was an entirely involuntary action on my part. Some women are made to be hugged and Megan is one of them. She looked startled and I patted her shoulder to make the hug seem something a good friend would do. And maybe it was.

She shook off my hand and stepped to the door to glance down the hall for any sight of Clyde Brownleigh. "I wish he would hurry up. I'm getting nervous again."

"He'll be here," I said with all the confidence in the world. "He came all this way to be the star of the show. Would he miss it?"

I had hardly finished speaking when Brownleigh walked through the door carrying a yellow legal pad and nothing else that I could see. His forehead was wrinkled above his hairy eyebrow, and I noticed that sweat gleamed on the back of his neck. He stalked to the podium and picked up the microphone. Instantly, video cameras sprouted from shoulders and eyeballs.

"I'm sorry."

These were not the words the audience had come to hear.

"Sorry for what?"

"Where's your string?"

"Aren't you going to demonstrate the Nauru Island figures?"

"What are you trying to pull?" demanded Randal Anderson. "Do you have the lost Jayne manuscript or not?"

Leave it to Randal to get to the bottom of the manure pile.

"Yes, I do," said Brownleigh, "but I won't own it much longer."

"Young man, what are you talking about?" shouted Dr. Moser.

"I just received a phone call from my wife. My mother fell and broke her hip this afternoon. She has no medical insurance and is too young to qualify for Medicare. I must sell the Jayne manuscript, and I cannot sell it to a commercial or academic press. Let's be realistic. A book on string figures, even one by Caroline Furness Jayne, will never make the *New York Times* Bestseller List, so no publisher will pay much for the manuscript. However, those of you in this room will. Therefore, however much I dislike it, I will sell the manuscript to the highest bidder in a silent auction. I will be in my hotel room this afternoon and this evening until twelve o'clock. I will again accept appointments from nine until eleven in the morning. I am leaving this legal pad on the podium. It is marked off in fifteen-minute units. You may sign up for a fifteen-minute examination of the manuscript, after which you may write your bid on a slip of paper I will provide and seal it in an envelope, which I also shall provide. I will open the sealed bids tomorrow at noon and will announce the winner. I will accept money orders, cashier's checks, or cash. How the highest bidder manages to arrange for one of the three acceptable methods of payment is not my concern. That is all I have to say."

With those final words, Brownleigh stepped away from the podium and vanished through a service door.

The room was silent for approximately ten seconds, then pandemonium reigned. In all my years as an academic, I have never witnessed such behavior. I saw Dr. Moser swinging his cane around with every intention of doing bodily harm to anyone who got in his way. Those who did either got swatted on their shins or their more manly parts, depending on gender. I saw Denise LeClerc shoving Randal Anderson, who didn't hesitate to shove back. What shocked me most was the sight of the Reverend Robert Wilson, an Anglican missionary to the Aborigines of the Northern Territory of Australia, joining forces with Rosemary and Lorene to clear a path to the podium. The reverend swung a briefcase while Rosemary and Lorene put a top spin on their purses that mowed down the opposition, that is, those without the sense to get out of the way. There is no force of nature more dangerous than two little old ladies intent on a goal. Add a clergyman to the mix, and I'd rather face Hurricane Andrew.

I was so mesmerized by the pushing and shoving, the blows exchanged, the rattle of such weapons as briefcases, canes, tackle boxes full of string, that I nearly missed a glimpse of curly red hair. Megan was easily the shortest person in the room, so I would have lost sight of her altogether except that red hair is hard to miss. She was sliding along the wall, avoiding the worst of the combat areas, that intent expression on her face that says her goal is in sight and woe unto he who gets in her way. That's usually me. Remember it's Dr. Watson who always brings the revolver.

I slid along the wall after her, stiff-arming anyone who got too close, and caught her just as she reached the podium and the yellow legal pad. I picked her up and slung her over my shoulder, slipped out the same service door through which Brownleigh disappeared, and dropped her to the floor. I grabbed a chair and wedged it under the doorknob. I planned on chewing out Megan, and I didn't want the string-figure terrorists swarming through the door until I was done.

"What the devil did you think you were doing, Megan? Do you have some kind of a death wish? There must be some kind of poison gas blowing through the vents into that room because those people—and I'm including you—are crazy! If there isn't blood flowing yet, it's only a matter of time until it does. What possessed you to want to sign up to examine that manuscript? You couldn't afford it if it was on clearance at Wal-Mart."

Megan waved the legal pad at me. "I am signing up, Ryan, and be damned to you! I want to examine that manuscript. If I can cite Jayne's lost manuscript as a source, I *know* I can sell an article on string figures to the *Smithsonian* or even *National Geographic*. I'll be a legitimate scholar instead of a beggar at the doors of the snooty journals. I worked so hard for my education, and I can't use any of it in my present situation. I sense my knowledge, my skills, slipping away from me. I'm not even a full-fledged reference librarian. I'm just an assistant."

To my horror, Dr. Megan Elizabeth Clark, Ph.D.

in physical anthropology with a specialty in paleo-pathology, burst into tears.

"Let me have the damn legal pad, Megan. I'll write your name down to examine the manuscript, then I'll open the door and throw the legal pad back into the Sagebrush Room. Then, after I make a phone call, I'm taking you to the bar and buying you the biggest margarita the bartender can make. In fact, I might buy you two."

She sniffed and wiped her eyes on the tail of her convention T-shirt. "Who are you going to call?"

"Nine-one-one. I figure we're going to need the paramedics to treat the wounded."

5

The worst of the man is, he has a method. He doesn't go out of his way to cheat us; he makes us go out of ours to be cheated.

—SIR CHARLES VANDRIFT OF COLONEL CLAY
in Grant Allen's "The Episode of the
Diamond Links," *An African Millionaire*, 1897

Megan swallowed the last of her second margarita and sat her glass down. Next to her, Ryan drank the last of his rum and Coke.

"May I have the honor of buying you and Dr. Megan Clark another drink, Dr. Stevens?" asked the gentleman on Ryan's left at the large round table in the darkest corner of the High Plains Motel's Cactus Bar.

"I regret that I must limit myself to one drink, Dr. Yahara. Not that I'm an alcoholic, but I'm allergic to brewer's yeast. One drink I can tolerate. Two, and I'm sick. As for Dr. Clark, she has already slurped up two very large margaritas. Another one and she would develop a case of giggles," said Ryan.

"I do not giggle," said Megan. "I am Celtic to the bone and was born knowing how to hold my liquor."

"You may hold your liquor, but you still giggle," said Ryan. "I don't think I'm up to giggles tonight.

In fact, I'm not up to much tonight. I haven't recovered from the brouhaha this afternoon. Am I the only person out of this whole convention who doesn't want to buy the Caroline Furness Jayne manuscript?"

"You may be, laddie," said Dr. Moser, sporting a black eye and three stitches just above his right eyebrow where the metal catch on Rosemary's purse had caught him as the two of them both lunged for the legal pad at the same time. "For myself, I want it very badly. It was written by the only woman I ever loved. She was beautiful as an angel and as kind as one, too. Her father, brothers, husband, and son never overcame their grief at losing her. I didn't either. I remember the evening my mother told me that Caroline Furness Jayne had died. I cried myself to sleep that night. It doesn't matter that I was barely four, or was I five? I loved her like no woman I ever married. Went through three wives hunting for a woman like her—or half as good as her. Even named my eldest daughter Caroline. What would I give for her lost manuscript? I'd pay my last dime and give up my firstborn—if he wasn't sixty-five years old and a professor of physics at MIT. As it is, money will have to do. I suspect it's all Brownleigh's interested in, and I have enough of it to satisfy his greed."

"Then you don't believe his story about his mother's broken hip?" asked Megan.

"My lovely young lady, I taught at the University of Pennsylvania for nearly fifty years, in fact, the board of regents had to force me into retirement, and I have heard the old 'grandmother's operation' story with all its endless variations more times than I want to remember. If Mr. Brownleigh even has a mother instead of springing full-grown from pond scum, I would be surprised. No, my dear, Mr. Brownleigh planned to auction off that manuscript all along, so don't waste any sympathy on his imaginary mother and her broken hip."

He turned to Dr. Yahara. "Tomoyuki, as two of the founding members of the International String Figure Association, I think we should have the honor of buying one another a drink." He turned to Megan, his faded blue eyes twinkling. "My dear Miss Megan, have you and Dr. Stevens had the privilege of a formal introduction to Dr. Tomoyuki Yahara, professor of mathematics, and a member of Nippon Ayatori Kyokai, otherwise known as the String Figure Association of Japan?"

Megan wasn't sure how she liked being called Miss Megan. It was the sort of address used by Dr. Moser's generation for either a very young girl or a spinster. She wondered which one he thought she was.

"We've not been formally introduced, no, Dr. Moser," said Megan. "But Ryan and I have enjoyed his company without a formal introduction. I hope you haven't thought us too forward, Dr. Yahara."

"No, no," said Yahara vehemently. "When in Rome, I believe the saying goes. When in Texas, one must be very much informal."

"So tell us, Dr. Yahara, why do you want the manuscript?" asked Ryan. Megan felt like kicking him.

There was informal, and then there was nosy. In her opinion, Ryan had crossed the line.

Dr. Yahara signaled the waitress for another round of drinks before Megan could stop him. Oh, well, what was a case of giggles between friends.

The Japanese professor folded his hands against his chest in a formal gesture. "Why do I want the lost manuscript, Dr. Stevens? That is a difficult question to answer. I am the most well-known string-figure enthusiast in Japan. I am asked to demonstrate string figures to children in classrooms, and to businessmen in boardrooms. To have the opportunity to obtain the Jayne manuscript, and not to do so, is not acceptable to me. I am prepared to risk my family's export business in cultured pearls to buy the manuscript. It is a matter of face, Dr. Megan Clark, a word that equates to your concept of honor, but is much stronger. I must have the manuscript."

Ryan leaned close and whispered in Megan's ear. "His bowl of rice is a few grains short of full, or there is something he's not telling us."

"Like what?"

"I don't know, but I don't believe we're hearing the whole story from anybody."

"I'm usually the cynical one, Ryan."

"Not this time. As the only person who doesn't want the manuscript, I'm the only objective observer, and it's my objective observation that everyone is a brick shy of a full load when it comes to that lost manuscript."

"Naughty, naughty, mustn't whisper," said Dr.

Moser. "Unless you are whispering sweet nothings in her lovely ear, Dr. Stevens."

"Just telling her not to get her hopes up about the manuscript. An assistant librarian's salary can't compete with an export business, nor with your inherited wealth, Dr. Moser."

"You mustn't be such a pessimist. Perhaps Brownleigh will choose to give the prize to beauty instead of us beasts."

"From my short acquaintance with Brownleigh, I don't see that happening. He didn't strike me as much of a romantic."

"I have the honor of agreeing with you, Dr. Stevens," said Dr. Yahara. "Mr. Brownleigh is a very cold man. He would not warm himself at the altar of beauty."

"This is a disgusting and humiliating conversation," said the only other woman besides Megan sitting at the table. "You all talk about beauty like it was all that a woman had to offer. What if a woman is ugly? What then? Would you men still tease *Dr. Clark* with your quasi-sexual remarks if she had a harelip or a crooked leg or one eye smaller than the other?"

"But she isn't ugly or malformed, and if she were, we would still be kind to her," said Dr. Moser in a mild tone of voice.

"Kind? Kind? That is your answer to millennia of humiliating, browbeating, and dominating women? You are kind to animals. Women deserve more."

"Please, Ms. LeClerc, let us enjoy our drinks with-

out one of your lectures on how brutish men are,"
said a sunburned, balding young man dressed in
Levi's, a convention T-shirt, and turquoise jewelry.
"I didn't come to the convention to dominate anyone."

"I agree," said Dr. Moser. "I've had all the con-
frontation I can tolerate today."

Denise LeClerc, social anthropologist and radical
feminist, pushed back her chair and stood up. She
was a tall woman with a poorly defined waist and no
makeup of any kind, as if any attempt at beautifying
herself was a betrayal of her principles. Megan wondered why every radical feminist she knew equated
makeup with betrayal of the cause. There must be
some connection she was missing.

"I will confront Brownleigh tonight," said Denise.
"I have one of the last appointments. I want the manuscript for the Museum of Women's Achievements.
Caroline Furness Jayne was a remarkable woman, an
intellectual whose sex prevented her from receiving
the credit due her for her first book on string figures.
If Brownleigh weren't such a pig, he would donate
the manuscript instead of holding us up for money."

"I think if you squeeze Brownleigh, he will oink,"
said Ryan.

"That's the first sensible thing you've said tonight,
Dr. Stevens. Too bad most of your conversation isn't
so clever."

With that remark, Denise LeClerc marched toward
the door, shoulders squared as though she were in a
military parade.

The balding young man expelled a loud breath. "My mother tried to raise me to be a gentleman, but my mother never met Denise LeClerc. That is the most unpleasant young woman I've ever met, and I keep meeting her at every anthropology seminar I attend. One of these days I'm going to say something very crude that will justify all the bad opinions of men that Denise holds, but you know what? When that day comes, I'm going to enjoy it. Oh, excuse me, I'm John Harper," he said, rising to shake hands with everyone at the table. "I'm an anthropologist specializing in the study of the Pueblo Indian culture of the American Southwest, and I wrote my master's thesis on string figures. I'm gathering evidence to support a sort of unified field theory in string-figure art, that certain techniques are universal and represent a commonality of experience. My conclusions will be the basis for my doctoral dissertation, and I expect Jayne's lost manuscript to support my theories. I inherited some property and money from my parents, and I will spend all of it on Jayne's manuscript."

"A unified field theory of string figures," said Megan, trying to keep from yawning. People whose conversation sounded like they were reading from their thesis always made her sleepy. "That's an interesting idea."

"If you will excuse me, it's close to my appointment time. I don't want to lose a minute's opportunity to examine the manuscript. I hope to see you all later."

"Not if I see him first," said Ryan under his breath

to Megan. "You know, Einstein couldn't prove his unified field theory in physics where there's a yes-or-no answer to every question. How will Harper prove his theory in an art form whose every figure has variations? Besides, I don't think his brain power has the necessary wattage to compete with Einstein's."

"Ah, whispering more sweet nothings," said Dr. Moser. "Much more of that and you must tell us all what you said. Would that shock you, Reverend Wilson?"

The Reverend Robert Wilson, last seen battling his way toward the podium with Rosemary and Lorene, smiled and shook his head. "Dr. Moser, in my profession I hear the most cruel remarks that one human could make about another. Sweet nothings would be a welcome change."

"You are a missionary to the Aborigines, Reverend Wilson?" asked Megan. "Have you collected many string figures from that culture?"

"Oh, yes, Dr. Clark. I'm an avid collector of string figures from isolated and primitive cultures, and I'm desperate to obtain the Jayne manuscript because Brownleigh claims that it includes instructions from original sources for making the string figures of Nauru Island, the most complicated and intricate and beautiful string figures known to exist. I examined the manuscript earlier this evening, but he would only let me see one page of the Nauru Island material."

"Would someone explain to me what is so unique about these Nauru Island string figures?" asked Ryan. Megan wondered why he was asking that question, since the answer was in one of her articles that she read to him not more than a month ago.

"I would be glad to," said Reverend Wilson. "Nauru Island is a tiny piece of land only eight-point-two square miles with a population of eighteen hundred or so. It was overrun by the Japanese during the Second World War, and a majority of its population was deported to Truk Island as slave labor to build an airstrip. Nearly half died on Truk. Although those still alive were repatriated to Nauru after the war, the Nauru culture was changed beyond repair. Apparently none of the string-figure masters survived, so instructions from original sources were no longer available. That portion of Nauru culture was dead, never to be revived. If the Jayne manuscript includes instructions for reconstructing those lost string figures, it would be a find of major anthropological significance. It is unspeakable for Mr. Brownleigh to sell—*sell*—the Jayne manuscript for thirty pieces of silver."

"I agree with you, Reverend," said an untidy young man whose very appearance screamed "Geek!" "My name is David Owen Lister, and I own a business in cyberspace called the Hobby Emporium. I sell all kinds of materials necessary to hobbies, such as special paper for those who are into origami. I also sell string to you enthusiasts. When I win the silent auction, I will immediately set the manuscript in type and publish it. With a monopoly on distribution, I could ask any price I choose, but I don't care about money. I care about being needed."

"That term is a euphemism for a thirst for power," whispered Ryan.

Megan stood up and gathered the backpack she carried instead of a purse. "Take me home, Ryan. Tomorrow will be another busy day."

Ryan looked surprised, but hurried along beside her. "What's the matter, honey?"

Megan caught the endearment, and knew that soon she and Ryan would have to talk about their relationship. It seemed to be shifting under Megan's feet like sand. But that wasn't what was bothering her now.

"They all have an agenda, Ryan. It's like nobody is thinking of the manuscript as a treasure that belongs to everybody. This is Caroline Furness Jayne's dying gift to the world, and nobody sees it that way. Not even me. I just thought of using it to make money, so I guess I'm no better than the rest of them."

"Megan! There is nothing wrong with earning a little money writing articles. Even Dickens wrote for money."

"Never mind trying to make me feel better about myself, Ryan. I have the soul of a robber baron and never knew it until tonight."

6

CHEATING THE HANGMAN

A string trick originally collected from the Philippines, but also found in Japan. One should take care if performing this trick.

1. Hang the loop of string around your neck.

2. Wrap the right string of the loop once around your neck.

3. Make Position 1, then Opening A with the strings of the hanging loop.

4. Drop Loop L5 and Loop R5 (drop loops on Left and Right Little Fingers) and extend.

5. Insert from below the R3, 4, and 5 into the Loop R2 (insert from below the Middle, Ring, and Little Fingers into the Loop around the Index Finger). Repeat movements for the L3, 4, and 5.

6. Close L2, 3, 4, and 5 (Left Index, Middle, Ring, and Little Fingers) and R2, 3, 4, and 5 (Right Index, Middle, Ring, and Little Fingers) on F1 (Far Thumb String) and N1 (Near Index Finger).

7. Your string loop now has one string at the top, and two strings at the bottom. Turn the string loop upside down so there are two strings at the top and one string at the bottom of your loop.

8. Put your head through the loop held by your hands.

9. Let go of your string loop and it will hang around your neck and down your chest. With L2 and R2 (Left and Right Index Fingers) gently pull out the sides of this loop and the string will come free. DO NOT YANK ON THE STRING IF IT FAILS TO DROP FREE. THIS COULD BE DANGEROUS.

I was shocked. No, more than shocked by Megan's dark mood. She hardly ever is blue, and I worried all night about her. Maybe it was one of those hormonal things that women (according to my late wife) suffer occasionally, and that we men shrug off with bad jokes. I don't think I've ever been guilty of that—three of my four children are female, which pretty well cured me of making any PMS jokes—but perhaps Megan wasn't feeling up to her usual disgustingly healthy self. Being nineteen years older than she—well, maybe a bit more than that—I occasionally suffer a stiff joint or my knees make creaking sounds, or getting up isn't as easy as it used to be, and I certainly never was a member of the University of Texas varsity women's crew, so my conditioning even when I was Megan's age was never likely to inspire makers of the various exercise equipment to ask me to whip off my shirt and endorse their products. What I'm getting at is that Megan Clark is a poster child for both physical and mental health. Mention depression to her, and she immediately thinks of a dip in whatever dirt road she may be driving her black behemoth GMC pickup.

I was worried enough about her that I offered to drive my white Ford Ranger to the High Plains Motel so she wouldn't have to deal with the morning rush-hour traffic on I-40. Not that Amarillo has much rush-hour traffic on I-40 or any other street or highway, but I thought she just might like to be a passenger instead of a driver. I confess I had another motive as well. Megan is so short that it is almost impossible to sit beside her when she's driving, because the seat is pushed as close to the steering wheel as design will allow, and I have to sit sideways with my knees practically under my chin. And that is only one way in which riding with Megan Clark is an adventure. Let me just say that I was glad to drive her instead of the reverse.

"Ryan?"

"Yes?"

"I've decided that I was being stupid last night."

"I didn't want to call—"

"I've decided that writing an article for the *Smithsonian* or *National Geographic* about the lost manuscript would be a way of honoring Caroline Furness Jayne."

"I think I tried to tell—"

"Not because of anything Denise LeClerc said, because most of it was wrong—Jayne was highly thought of by the anthropologists of her time—but because there are new generations who need to learn of her work."

"I think that's an excellent—"

"And to make sure that my motives are pure, I will donate my fee to anthropological research at the University of Pennsylvania. That's where so many members of her family taught."

"Now that's the first stupid thing you've said, Megan. Do you believe that a woman like Caroline Furness Jayne would expect a struggling anthropologist slash archaeologist to give up her fee? I don't think so."

Megan looked at me out of those pale whiskey-brown eyes that are so striking with her copper-colored hair. Sometimes I lose track of what she's saying because I'm so absorbed in admiring her unusual eyes and hair. That wasn't the case this morning, however, as her eyes had what I called her 180-proof expression.

"I don't know how you can be so sure, since you never even heard of the woman until six weeks ago when I started discussing my articles with you."

"Intuition?"

"Hey, this is an ethnic Celt you're talking to. We invented intuition. Not that I would depend on it in any serious situation. I like my intuition based on scientific fact." She poked my arm. "Let me off at the front door. My appointment is right after Dr. Moser's and I don't want to be late."

I let her off, a morose little figure in her khaki carpenter pants with all the pockets, her convention T-shirt, and the black backpack she carried through Europe the year she studied at the University of Glasgow. I often wondered what the real Celts thought of their American cousin. Judging from the number of e-mails she still received from her classmates at Glasgow, those hairy-legged Scots and Irishmen, and even the occasional Englishman, remembered her with fondness. Megan Clark has a bit of Caroline Furness Jayne's charisma although I doubt she knew it, or would admit it if she did.

I parked my Ranger near the front door in case I needed to make a quick getaway—from what I don't know, but after yesterday's Battle of the Sagebrush Room, I wanted to be prepared to make a strategic withdrawal if necessary. I'm no George Armstrong Custer. Last stands aren't my style.

I stopped at the restaurant and bought a large coffee—black, no sugar—and strolled past the motel swimming pool on my way to Brownleigh's room. I thought I might as well wait as close to the action as possible, and I figured Brownleigh's room would be the source of whatever action there was.

I was barely halfway down the hall when I heard the commotion. At first I thought I was about to witness the Battle of the Lost Manuscript, and debated whether I should make that strategic withdrawal I mentioned before, when I remembered that Megan was in harm's way. Or many of the enthusiasts were in Megan's way, which might be more serious, so I jogged the remainder of the way to Brownleigh's room.

Dr. Moser was sitting against the wall beside Brownleigh's closed door, with Rosemary fanning him with her convention program, while Lorene patted his face with a damp hankie and Randal Anderson generally hovered without doing anything useful. But what really provided impetus for my heart to drop to my knees was that Megan Clark was nowhere to be seen.

"Where's Megan? Has anyone seen Megan? Is she hurt? I warn you, Dr. Moser, if this is another one of those disgraceful shoving matches like yesterday afternoon, I'm closing this convention down and partially refunding everyone's money."

"Megan's fine, Ryan," said Lorene. "And I think it's too late to close down the convention. We might as well go ahead with the workshops since the police will keep everyone here anyway. At least, we can keep our minds off what happened if we're in a workshop. I'm particularly interested in the string figures of Africa, because I wonder if Agatha Christie ever saw any of them when she was on a dig in Iraq or Iran or Egypt with her husband. Or did her husband ever do any excavations in Egypt? I can't remember. But he must have when you consider the number of mysteries she wrote with an Egyptian setting. But I'm not the Christie authority, Rosemary is.

Did you ever read *Come, Tell Me How You Live,* her book about living at a dig?"

"You really should read it," said Rosemary. "It's very humorous, particularly the section on her renting a cat to get rid of the mice. Or was it rats? Do you remember, Lorene? Was it mice or rats?"

"What are you two talking about, and what is wrong with Dr. Moser, and where in the hell is Megan?"

Rosemary frowned at me. "It isn't necessary to use profanity, Ryan. We'll tell you where Megan is. In fact, she told us to, and to tell you to call the police."

"Rosemary, look at me. Let's start at the beginning. Where is Megan?"

"She's in with the body, of course. You don't expect Dr. Moser to sit with it, do you? He's a mathematician and has no experience with bodies, plus he's getting on in years and isn't as resilient as when he was younger."

My heart, which had already dropped to my knees, continued its descent to the vicinity of my ankles. I tried to talk, but my mouth had dried out. I took a gulp of coffee and managed to generate enough spit to ask in a hoarse whisper, "What body?"

"Why, Clyde Brownleigh's, of course," answered Lorene. "Whose did you think we were talking about?"

I found enough saliva to laugh hysterically until I realized how laughter at a crime scene must look to people who don't know me. "What happened?" I finally gasped out the words, but by this time even

Rosemary and Lorene were looking at me with disapproval in their blue eyes.

"They already told you, Ryan," said Randal Anderson, squatting down beside Dr. Moser and taking his pulse—like Randal knew how to take a pulse. Or maybe he did. "Clyde Brownleigh bit the big weenie. He's deader than the proverbial doornail."

"But what happened?" I demanded.

Dr. Moser stirred to life, or as much of it as he could still claim at ninety-six. "Murder, young Dr. Stevens, blackhearted murder—although blackhearted describes the victim as well as the murderer, so maybe I shouldn't be so judgmental."

I slid down the wall to join Dr. Moser on the floor. "Maybe it was a heart attack."

"Young man, at my age I've seen most of my friends suffer heart attacks—seen most of them die, for that matter—but I've never seen one who looks like Clyde Brownleigh. It's murder, all right. I knew that without ever having seen a murder victim in my life. All I can say is that I hope he gets a good undertaker, because he's going to need one, or it'll be a closed-casket funeral."

I tried not to imagine what Brownleigh might look like. "A man has been murdered, and all of you are making jokes about it?"

"It's not that Lorene and I, and Dr. Moser and Randal don't disapprove of the act of murder, Ryan, because we do, but Mr. Brownleigh was a very unpleasant young man, and excessive grief seems hypocritical under the circumstances," said Rosemary.

"Besides, we just discovered the body—or rather Dr. Moser did—only a few minutes ago, and I suspect we're using black humor to keep away the horror, don't you, Rosemary?" asked Lorene.

"Most of our mysteries speak of using black humor for just that purpose, Lorene, so I think we're following a tradition," replied Rosemary.

The first time I met Rosemary and Lorene—"the twins," as Megan calls them, although they aren't related—they reminded me of the two sisters in *Arsenic and Old Lace*. Sometimes they still do. "Have you called the police at least?"

"Megan said to wait and let you call Lieutenant Carr, because he always believes you more than her," said Lorene.

Not until Lorene mentioned Lieutenant Jerry Carr—a former student of mine and some twelve or thirteen years younger—did the whole mess suddenly take shape and sink into my psyche. Murder! How did this happen?

"I'm sure it was greed, young man," said Dr. Moser, sitting up straighter with his color much improved from the gray it had been when I first saw him.

"What are you talking about?"

"You asked how this happened, and I told you: greed. I would think that greed on the part of either the victim or the murderer would be the most likely motive for most—uh—killings."

"I must have been thinking out loud, because I don't remember saying anything. I was just trying to work out in my mind how the Murder by the Yard Reading Circle could possibly be in the vicinity of murder again."

"Actually, it's not the reading circle, Ryan, old boy; it's your significant companion in there," said Randal. "She's messing about with another corpse."

Lieutenant Jerry Carr of the Potter-Randall-Armstrong Counties Special Crimes Unit, hereafter referred to as Special Crimes, is what my mother used to call a "tall drink of water." He's over six feet, and good-looking in a square-jawed, Dick Tracy sort of way. You may think I'm being prejudiced, and you would be right. Jerry Carr has—or is—sometimes keeping company with Megan Clark, although their relationship has cooled off since he suspected her of murder last spring. I remind Megan of his lack of faith at every opportunity, not because I'm a cruel man, but because I'm the older man in this triangle of sorts, and need all the breaks I can get. I'm certain there's an intimacy between them—or was an intimacy, although I don't believe it was more blatantly sexual than a kiss. Megan has places to go and mummies to see, and she has no intention of entering into any romantic entanglements. I do my best to help her avoid them.

Jerry Carr was making a sort of generalized announcement to the group and its subject was Megan Clark. "How can one female, even if she is Megan Clark, be involved in more than one murder in a lifetime? We're not talking about a policewoman, or a member of the FBI or the intelligence services, or even the armed services. She's a librarian, for God's sake! It defies mathematical probability!"

Megan didn't bother to respond—which worried me.

"Oh, we don't know that for certain, young man. Now give me the actual numbers of innocent young women who find themselves involved in some way with murder, remembering to include wives, mothers, and sisters of both the victims and the murderers, and the actual number of reported homicides in the United States, and I will give you the probability. It is probably higher than you assume," said Dr. Moser, leaning against the wall and sipping what looked to Ryan like a very large bourbon and water.

"And who are you?" asked Jerry, opening a small spiral notebook.

"I am Dr. Solomon Moser, professor emeritus of mathematics at the University of Pennsylvania, and I actually discovered the body."

"Don't go running off until I talk to you."

"At my age, when I move at all, it is never at a run, so you may assume I will be right here or in the hospitality room or the bar whenever you desire a conversation with me, Lieutenant," said Dr. Moser, saluting the head of Special Crimes with his bourbon and water.

I had anticipated Jerry Carr's next movement before he made it, and I was right. He turned to Megan and glared down at her. Being Megan, she glared right back at him, thank God. It meant she was on the road to recovery of her basic personality: stubborn determination, Generation-X variety.

"I don't find bodies on purpose, Jerry. At least, fresh ones."

"And you've been messing around with the corpse, haven't you? When are you going to learn to keep your nose out of police business?"

"When you learn that I have the best damn nose in the entire Panhandle to stick into a murder investigation."

"What would your mother think if she heard even the mildest profanity coming out of your mouth?"

"If you want profanity, you ought to hear what comes out of *her* mouth. We're talking about the woman who backed down the Department of Energy when they planned to put a high-level nuclear waste dump in the Panhandle. *And* don't tell me how to behave!"

Jerry Carr and Megan were standing practically nose to nose, screaming at each other, and I, forgive me, was enjoying myself.

Suddenly Megan stepped back. "Can we argue another time, Jerry? I am the one most qualified not only to recognize the uniqueness of the murder weapon, but to reconstruct how the murder occurred. Will you let me help? Or will you let a murderer walk?"

"What is so unique about the weapon that no one else but you would recognize it?" demanded Jerry.

"The murder weapon is a string figure called Cheating the Hangman."

7

*Murderers, in general, are people who are consistent,
people who are obsessed with one idea and nothing
else. And that applies to their victims, as well.*

—THE NOTARY in Ugo Betti's
Struggle Till Dawn, Act 1, 1949;
English translation by G. H. McWilliam, 1964

Megan took a deep breath before stepping back inside Clyde Brownleigh's room. Ryan, and for that matter, everyone in the Murder by the Yard Reading Circle, believed that dead bodies didn't bother her.

That wasn't true. A mummy, or other long-dead corpse didn't bother her, because she had never known "him" alive. He only lived in a world of virtual reality, one she created for him from her knowledge and imagination so she might better see the shrunken, darkened body before her as alive and full of earthly juices, ready to confess how the life he lived marked his guts and bones with disease and injuries.

She had known Clyde Brownleigh. Maybe not well, but she had watched him eat, walk, laugh—if insincerely—a fully functional human being. It didn't matter that she didn't like him; he was alive, moving, breathing. Death is irreversible. Once life is gone, you can never call it back.

She felt Jerry Carr's arm around her shoulders. "It's okay, Megan. I'm with you."

She looked up at him and recognized the expression in his eyes. He knew, *knew* what she was feeling, because he had felt it, too. Once you have known the intimacy of life, it's difficult to achieve cold objectivity toward one who departed prematurely and violently.

She nodded and stepped inside Brownleigh's room and walked across the beige carpet to the small desk in front of which the corpse sat in an upholstered armchair. Lips and ears a purple-blue color, a bloody froth about his mouth and nostrils, tongue protruding like a thick piece of beef, hands clenched, Clyde Brownleigh was not a pretty sight. The classic signs of asphyxiation—tiny hemorrhages or petechia—speckled his neck and face above the ligature. Megan knew that if she looked into his eyes, the petechia would be even more prominent.

She didn't look. There was no need. There could be no question that this was murder, because the murderer had left his weapon, a yellow woven cord wrapped tightly around the victim's neck and tangled in his hands.

"It's called Cheating the Hangman," said Megan, not liking the toneless quality she could hear in her own voice. It was a symptom of emotional shock, a state she knew she was very close to, but had no intention of actually falling into. "It's a string trick, which, if done correctly, allows the cord to fall harm-lessly from the neck. If done improperly—well, I doubt anyone would accidently strangle himself. Self-preservation is generally too strong to allow such an accident. Still, improperly done, Cheating the Hangman could give you a good scare."

"But you don't think this was an accident?" asked Jerry, staring at the corpse.

"No. See how the loop is pulled so tightly around the neck that it actually cuts into the flesh under the chin? That tells me that someone stood behind Brownleigh and tightened the loop with—something, some object that could be inserted inside the loop to twist it even tighter, a ballpoint, a piece of silverware, even a pencil. And the hands, look at his hands, Jerry. They are clenched, with the string looped loosely around them. If this were an accident, we would see the opposite. The hands would be clenched around the cord so tightly that the creases of the fingers would be cut."

Megan backed away until she bumped into the door, then took one step forward so she wouldn't be plastered against it like some heroine from a fifties horror movie. She wasn't *afraid* of a corpse. She was no fading pansy or dying lily or whatever the ex-pression was; she had just had enough of death.

"This is murder, and your pathologist will agree with me when he does the autopsy. And the cord?" She swallowed again, her mouth dry. "David Owen Lister, the guy who owns the cyberspace hobby shop, sells string exactly like that, and nearly everyone at

the convention bought some because it's such an unusual color, sort of a sunflower yellow. It's one of us
at the convention who did this, one of us who knew
how to make the figure of Cheating the Hangman,
one of us who bought some of the yellow string, and
one of us who stole Caroline Furness Jayne's lost
manuscript."

Jerry held up his hand. "Whoa there, what lost
manuscript and who is Caroline Furness Jayne? Another conventioneer?"

"Please, let's go down the hall. I can feel Clyde
Brownleigh staring at me."

Jerry took her arm. "Me, too. Much more of looking at his tongue, and I'll convert to vegetarianism."

Megan followed him down the hall and into the
motel manager's office, a small cubbyhole of a room
with a desk, computer, and two chairs, one behind
the desk and one in front. Megan sank down in the
one in front, not because it looked more comfortable,
but because it was closest when she felt her legs turn
rubbery. Murder on top of organizing a convention
on top of a full-time job was asking too much of even
her stamina. And now she would have to deal with
all the questions from the enthusiasts, not to mention
Jerry Carr and his Special Crimes Unit. There were
moments—and this was one of them—when she
wished she hadn't grown up. Being an adult was not
all it was cracked up to be.

She drew a breath so deep, it nearly made her
light-headed. "First of all, let me tell you about Caroline Furness Jayne and string figures."

She watched his face as she gave him a mini-lesson on the history of string figures, and the strong passions the intricate folk art provoked.

"So, you think the manuscript is the motive?" asked Jerry.

"It has to be. Brownleigh was a stranger to the string-figure enthusiasts. It's a small group, they all know each other, but no one knew him. He introduced himself at the luncheon at noon yesterday, and by shortly after midnight he's dead. How could he make someone angry enough to kill him in twelve hours? Logically, he didn't, so hatred probably isn't the motive. The only thing he had that anybody wanted was the Jayne manuscript, and it's gone, so the murderer had to have taken it."

"Back up a minute. How do you know he was killed shortly after midnight?"

"I don't—exactly—since time of death is so hard to determine down to the minute—or hour, but his last appointment was at eleven forty-five with Denise LeClerc, and I doubt she killed him."

"Why not?" interrupted Jerry.

"She's a feminist of the most radical persuasion. If she had killed him, she would have made a statement out of the murder."

"Done a Bobbit on him?"

"Possibly, but there's another reason I don't think she's guilty. She wants the manuscript for a museum. If she killed Brownleigh, she wouldn't ever be able to display it in her museum without drawing suspicion on herself. Another thing, I don't think she'd risk prison for any man ever born."

"So in your opinion this LeClerc woman would kill a man if she thought she wouldn't get caught, but otherwise no?"

"I suppose that's true of most of us."

Jerry watched her a moment. "You're too cute to be a cynic, Megan."

She sat up and glared at him. "Are you trying to start a fight?"

"No, I'm trying to make you mad. I just don't know how to make you smile anymore, not since I came so close to arresting you for murder last spring. I don't want you blue, Megan. It's not your natural temperament, and it worries me. I think it worries your lovesick professor, too."

"Ryan's not lovesick and he's not my professor!"

"How did you know I was talking about Ryan?"

She swallowed, and struggled to bring her emotions under some kind of control. "I thought we were talking about murder, Jerry, not my feelings."

"Okay, let's get back to the subject, then. So how did you know this manuscript was missing?"

Megan felt her face turn hot and knew her complexion must match the red in her hair. She looked down at the floor. "Because I looked for it."

"You contaminated a crime scene, Megan?"

She cringed at the harsh tone of his voice, and looked up at him. "I was careful. I know how to search an archaeological site without destroying it. A crime scene is not much different. And I was inside the room anyway. Someone had to go in to make sure Brownleigh was dead. We couldn't just assume he was. You know that, Jerry."

"So what would you have done if you had found the manuscript, Megan."

She avoided his eyes while she struggled for an answer. Finally, she looked at him. "I don't know."

8

CLYDE BROWNLEIGH'S SCHEDULED APPOINTMENTS ON THE EVE OF HIS DEATH

FRIDAY EVENING
 9:00—Rosemary Pittman
 9:15—Lorene Getz
 9:30—Reverend Robert Wilson
 9:45—Dr. Solomon Moser
10:00—Dr. Tomoyuki Yahara
10:15—Randal Anderson
10:30—John Harper
10:45—Herbert Jackson III
11:00—Agnes Caldwell
11:15—David Owen Lister
11:30—Candi Hobbs
11:45—Denise LeClerc

SATURDAY MORNING
 9:00—Dr. Solomon Moser
 9:15—Dr. Megan Clark

I caught Megan as she left the manager's office. She looked somber, which is better than morose. "You're serious? Somebody used a string figure to murder Brownleigh?"

She nodded her head, all those curls bouncing like little copper springs. "Cheating the Hangman, only he didn't."

I walked along beside her to the convention hospitality room, a two-story job with a tiny kitchen and two balcony bedrooms. The wall facing the pool is two stories of glass with what is probably the world's most expensive drapes. I've noticed that any piece of fabric hanging in front of a window is twice as expensive if it's called a drape instead of a curtain, and it's at least ten times as expensive if it's longer than fifty-four inches. I found that out when I had to replace my living-room drapes after tripping and dumping chili on them. They might not have required replacing if Megan's beagle, Rembrandt, hadn't shredded them trying to lick off the chili. Rembrandt has an evil mind. He uses my lawn as an outdoor toilet instead of Megan's; he growls at me as if he suspects me of dishonorable intentions toward his goddess; and he barks if I step out on my own front porch. I suspect he deliberately tripped me, knowing I was carrying a bowl of chili.

But to get back to the hospitality room, appropriately named by Megan the Apache Door, there were all the usual suspects milling around, meaning all the string-figure enthusiasts who wanted Jayne's manuscript, plus the Murder by the Yard Reading Circle. Megan and I were the exceptions, since we were together in a pickup on I-40 driving back home at approximately the time the murder occurred. In other words, we alibied each other, which was not necessarily a good thing since Jerry Carr believed the "lovesick professor" would lie for Megan if the Lord himself were interrogating him. Lovesick professor! When Megan told me that, I was flabbergasted. I don't know where Jerry Carr got that idea.

A chorus of voices greeted Megan the moment she stepped inside the door.

"Megan! The manager wants to know if we are still planning to have the banquet."

"Megan! What about the workshop room? Another convention wants to book it if we're not going to use it."

"Megan! Should I cancel the buses to Palo Duro Canyon?"

"Megan! Ryan threatened to cancel the rest of the convention!"

"Excuse me, Dr. Megan Clark, but the gentleman officer handed me a document he called a search warrant. Should I call my embassy?"

This last was from Dr. Tomoyuki Yahara, but his was only the first of the string-figure conventioneers' voices to be heard.

"Hey, Dr. Clark, I got a cop at my booth who wants all my yellow cord. He's got a search warrant, all right, but I don't think he ought to be able to grab all my yellow cord. It's the best seller I got." David Owen Wister apparently hadn't heard that his yellow cord was a suspected murder weapon.

"Megan! Lieutenant Carr not only wants to search my book booth, he wants to search my entire bookstore! I'll have to go with his investigators to clean up behind them while they search. Can you or Ryan keep my booth open while I'm gone?" Agnes Caldwell sounded frantic, and I didn't blame her. Just imagining Jerry Carr's boys loose in Time and Again Bookstore gave me a headache.

"Don't worry, Agnes, I'll see that it's taken care of. Candi, could you watch Agnes's booth? Randal, cancel the buses. Rosemary, tell the manager the banquet is still a go. Lorene, don't let the motel reassign our workshop room." She clapped her hands and raised her voice. "Listen, everybody, Ryan isn't going to cancel the rest of the convention, and if you will give me twenty minutes, I'll have a revised schedule posted."

"Megan. You might announce to everyone that I am a defense attorney and will be glad to answer any questions anyone has, as well as explain the search-warrant procedure to Dr. Yahara. All *pro bono* of course, unless someone is arrested, then I would have to start charging for my time." Herbert Jackson III pulled his denim vest down over his convention T-shirt, donned his denim jacket, and straightened his badge with *Host* stamped on it. Call Me Herb was all decked out in as close to the required three-piece-suit lawyer's uniform as any man could get during a weekend string-figure convention.

Megan and I always wondered if Herb wore a three-piece pajama suit to bed.

"Ah, a lawyer masquerading in false colors," said Dr. Moser, sitting on one of the three couches in the room with his feet propped on a square cocktail table and looking as wise as a man his age should look.

"But I for one am glad you are. It's always wise when dealing with the gendarmes to have an attorney present. A piece of advice my robber-baron grandfather gave me. Not that I am guilty, nor do I suspect any of you, but it's always best to observe the formalities."

"I want to talk to you first," said David Wister. "You got to get the cops out of my booth. They're scaring off my customers and taking all my yellow string."

"I don't think there is much Herb can do about that, David," said Megan, looking up from her position at the breakfast bar, where she was busily scribbling a revised schedule. "Your yellow cord was the murder weapon."

"They can't prove it's my yellow cord," protested David. "Can they?" His voice went from sounding indignant to plaintive.

Megan nodded. "I suspect they can. Special Crimes will send it to the FBI lab along with all the other yellow cord in everyone's possession, and compare the cut fibers on the end of each piece with fibers of the murder weapon. They'll find a match because I don't think it was a stranger who killed him, not since the Caroline Furness Jayne manuscript is missing—which I imagine is the second item listed on all the search warrants being served this morning. The third item is any knives or scissors you may have at your booth, David."

David Wister backed away, shaking his head so hard I wondered if it would fall off and roll under the cocktail table. "I never killed Brownleigh. No way. What good would it do me? I couldn't publish the Jayne manuscript if I killed him and stole it. The cops would throw me in jail before I could get the manuscript set in type."

"David, I'm not accusing you of killing Brownleigh. In fact, I know he was alive when you left him last night," said Megan.

"Ah, how do you know that, Dr. Megan Clark?" asked Dr. Yahara.

Megan shrugged. "Because I know Candi Hobbs and Denise LeClerc both had appointments after you. I assume that both of them would have noticed if Brownleigh had been strangled."

Candi Hobbs, a sweet girl and very bright, but not very socially adept—which may explain why she was in a relationship with Randal Anderson—shivered at Megan's words. "I would have screamed my head off if he had been dead."

"That's what's wrong with the feminine image," said Denise LeClerc. "Even women who pass for intelligent add to the stereotypical. Scream your head off. That's just what men expect us to do."

Randal rubbed his goatee and poked Denise's arm. "Know what? I'm not a woman, and I probably would have screamed my head off, too. Ever seen a strangled man, lady?"

"No, and don't call me lady."

"I haven't either, but I've read enough descriptions of strangulations to know that you ought not to be talking about a subject you don't know anything about."

"It is incorrect to end a sentence with a preposition," said Denise.

"How would you know?" asked Randal. "You're a social anthropologist."

"That's my avocation. My vocation is professor of English at Boston College."

Randal turned crimson and I actually felt sorry for him, because next to Denise LeClerc, Randal Anderson is affability itself. "Excuse me, I'm a professor of English, too, and I should have been more careful of my grammar. Let me rephrase that. You ought not to be talking about a subject you don't know anything about, *lady* !"

I thought it was Randal's finest hour.

Megan slid off her bar stool and climbed on the cocktail table, where she stood with her back to the glass wall and facing everyone in the room. "If I may have your attention, please."

She might as well have stayed at the bar, because Denise LeClerc went on talking as if Megan were a cute little grammar-school-age girl doing a pirouette on the cocktail table. "You are being insulting because as a woman with a superior degree and a superior teaching position, I am a threat to you."

Randal shoved his face close to Denise's. "You want to see insulting, you just try making another snide remark about Candi."

"Isn't that sweet?" asked Denise. "See the ape-man

defending his Jane—who ought to have the strength of character to defend herself."

"I think you've insulted Randal and me enough," said Candi as she seized a large pitcher of water and upended it on Denise's head. She sat the pitcher back on the cocktail table and stepped back to Randal's side. "How's that for strength of character?"

"SHUT UP!" shouted Megan.

You could have heard a pin drop in that room. Nothing is so shocking as when a short, sweet girl acts out of what most assume is her character. I knew better, of course, as did Lieutenant Jerry Carr, who had entered the room in time to see the altercation between Randal, Candi, and Denise. Megan Clark's tough-as-nails character did not match her exterior.

"Thank you for your attention," said Megan, her voice just faintly tinged with sarcasm. "In view of the murder and police requirements that we not leave the motel, we will reinstate the workshops beginning on the hour with the Life and Times of Caroline Furness Jayne. If you have your program, please scratch out Large-Loop String Figures, as we will not be going to Dick Bivins Stadium for a demonstration by the Boy Scouts. We will break for lunch today and tomorrow from twelve to one, and break for dinner at six to eight. I'm extending the Nauru Island Repertoire to two hours, and the Arctic String-Figure Project to three hours. The organizers of this convention can't be responsible for a registrant's missing a workshop or portion of a workshop due to having to give a statement to the police. I'll have the revised schedule copied and distributed shortly."

Megan had hardly climbed off the cocktail table when Jerry Carr strolled in the room.

"Very interesting conversations you folks have. Megan, how did you know the appointment times for Mr. Wister, Ms. Hobbs, and Dr. LeClerc? If you don't mind sharing the information, that is?"

Megan wrinkled her forehead and looked at Jerry a moment before replying. "I found the schedule in Brownleigh's room and copied it. This is my second murder, and I learn from experience. Always gather as much information as you can, because you never know when you may be the suspect."

Jerry Carr winced.

9

OSAGE TWO DIAMONDS

Caroline Furness Jayne learned this figure from an Osage Indian, Charles Michelle, at the St. Louis Exposition in September of 1904. The figure is also known in Hawaii.

1. Opening A.

2. Release Loop RI and Loop L1 (release the Right and Left Thumb Loops).

3. R1 and L1 (Right and Left Thumbs) over first three strings and pick up R5 Far and L5 Far and return (Right and Left Little Finger Far string and return Right and Left Thumbs to proper position).

4. With R1 and R2 (Right Thumb and Right Index Finger) pick up the L2 N string (Left Index Finger Near string) and place it over L1 (Left Thumb). Repeat on the Right Hand.

5. Navajo the Loop R1 and Loop L1 (lift the Lower Loop with the teeth over the Upper Loop and over the Right and Left Thumb).

6. Place the R2 and L2 (Right and Left Index Fingers) down into the triangles formed between

R1 and R2 and L1 and L2 (Right Thumb and
Right Index Finger, Left Thumb and Left Index
Finger), release R5 and L5 (Right and Left Little
Fingers), and turn the hands so the palms face
away from you, extending the R2 and L2 (Right
and Left Index Fingers) at the same time.

"I'm not surprised that somebody killed Brownleigh and stole the manuscript," said Ryan, tilting his
chair back against the wall in front of the Sagebrush
Room, where Dr. Solomon Moser, seemingly recovered from finding the grisly remains of Clyde Brownleigh, was lecturing on the Life and Times of
Caroline Furness Jayne.

"Why is that?" asked Megan. "Are you clairvoy-
ant?"

"No, but it's easy when you think about it. There
are too many ambitions resting on that manuscript,
and with all the string in every size for every purpose
in this motel, I'm not surprised somebody used it as
a murder weapon. This place is a smorgasbord for a
cult of Thugees looking for the latest thing in liga-
tures. Outside of a knife-and-gun show—and Amarillo won't host one of those until next February—I
can't think of a better place than a string-figure convention to pick up a handy murder weapon."

"Ryan, you're horrible!"

"I'm surprised you're not thinking the same thing.
You're the one who's always telling me I over-
estimate the goodness of the human race. Speaking
of murder and the human race, here comes Lieutenant

Jerry Carr himself." Ryan stretched out a foot, hooked another chair, and pulled it close to his and Megan's. "Take a load off, Jerry, and tell us what progress you've made toward finding the evil monster who strangled poor Clyde."

Jerry frowned at him and ignored the proffered chair. "You know I won't discuss an ongoing investigation, Doc."

Megan noticed Ryan glaring at Jerry. Ryan hated to be called Doc. Furthermore, Jerry knew it—which meant he did it deliberately—which meant the two men were acting like typical members of the male species in the presence of the female. If they had horns, both sets would already be locked together.

Sometimes Megan thought men were hopeless. Other times she knew they were.

"You won't find the manuscript," said Megan.

"How do you know that, Miss Female Sleuth? I haven't finished searching the motel yet. If it's here, I'll find it."

"Do I look like Nancy Drew or Miss Marple? Do you see me wearing pleated skirts and bobby socks, or carrying around a bag of knitting?"

"She dresses more like Kinsey Millhone," remarked Ryan.

"Ryan, you read a mystery!" exclaimed Megan.

"It was kind of an interesting book, because Kinsey Millhone reminds me a little of you. Not a lot, but enough to make me nervous if you happen to walk past a Volkswagen." He tilted his head to look up at the lieutenant. "Have you read *'A' Is for Alibi* by Sue Grafton, Jerry?"

"No, I guess I missed that one," replied the head of Special Crimes, his eyes narrowed until Megan wondered that he could see at all. She decided that Ryan had won that match, and it was time to step in before they started another.

"Jerry, this group of suspects—"

"They're not suspects yet!" he interrupted.

"Only because if you intimate in any way that any one of us is a suspect, you'll have to give us the Miranda warning and that brings in the lawyers— although Herb Jackson pretty well has all the defense business tied up in a package with a big red bow. But in your mind you're wondering which one of us did it."

"Okay, you tell me. Who killed Brownleigh and stole the manuscript?"

"You're assuming the same person did both."

Both men's jaws dropped open to the same forty-five-degree angle. Jerry recovered first. "What are you saying? You're the one who said the manuscript was the motive for the murder."

"Much as I hate agreeing with the lieutenant, he's right," said Ryan. "You did say that. And I agreed with you—not that I imagine it matters to Jerry."

Megan nibbled on her thumbnail, wondering why men always assumed women needed to be reminded of what they had said. If anything, it was the other way around. "I know what I said, and statistically I have at least a ninety percent chance of being right.

But what if I'm wrong? What if we are misled by the manuscript? By it's being missing, I mean."

"You're saying that one person killed him—for whatever reason—maybe they didn't like his wearing a corduroy suit in August—and somebody else showed up for his or her appointment, found him dead, and stole the manuscript?" asked Ryan. "That's a little thin, don't you think, Megan?"

"I suppose so, but I think that we ought to be really careful when we start assigning motive solely to the manuscript. The theft of same, I mean. Maybe we're supposed to think it's all about the manuscript. Maybe someone is trying to mislead us by making us believe that the most important aspect of the murder is the missing manuscript."

"What made you change your mind in the last hour, Megan?" asked the lieutenant, resting one foot on the chair and leaning his body on his raised knee. "I think you made more sense this morning. Of course, by your reasoning, no one killed Brownleigh, because each succeeding person with an appointment found him still alive. That's assuming that Dr. Denise LeClerc didn't kill him. What's your reasoning on her now that you've had a chance to think about it? Still think she wouldn't have killed him without mutilating the body to make some feminist statement?"

"She's too obvious a suspect," said Megan.

Jerry Carr slapped his knee and lifted his foot off the chair. He walked a few steps down the hall, paused, looked at the ceiling, cracked his knuckles several times, then walked back and stopped in front of Megan. "This is not one of your mysteries. This is morbid reality. This is a corpse with his tongue sticking out, on his way to Lubbock for an autopsy. This is not a game you and your reading circle can play while you have coffee and dessert!"

"Don't talk to me like I'm a silly woman. I know this isn't one of the mysteries that Murder by the Yard would spend the evening discussing. But on the other hand, maybe in a sense it is. These are not your usual suspects, Jerry. There are more Ph.D.s in this group than you will find at the average crime scene. Not that any of us are murderers, but if we were, I think we would all be very good at it. So I don't think the usual methods of detection will solve this crime. And I don't think that you're going to find that manuscript in this motel. Whoever stole it, is far too smart to leave it lying around."

"I wouldn't know because we're still searching. And by the way, I made your mother tie up that beagle of yours in the backyard. He kept trying to bite the two cops I sent to search your house," said Jerry.

"So, despite the fact that Ryan and I were driving home on I-40 at approximately the time of the murder, you're searching my house anyway?" asked Megan. She could feel her forehead wrinkling, a signal to anyone who knew her—and Jerry knew her—that she was royally provoked, and an explosion of some kind was imminent.

Jerry glanced away, his jaw clenching. Finally, he looked down at her. "I can't let you and the professor off the hook, any more that I can any of the convention registrants. According to that appointment list, nobody killed Brownleigh except maybe LeClerc, and you claim she didn't do it. Maybe he did get himself tangled up in that string figure—what's it called?"

"Cheating the Hangman."

"Yeah, Cheating the Hangman, that was it. So maybe he panicked and the more he tried to get out of the mess of string, the tighter it got, and he finally strangled himself. How do I know? The autopsy results won't be ready until tomorrow at the earliest."

"You know it wasn't an accident, Jerry," said Megan.

He ran his hands through his hair. "At this point I don't know anything, except I'll be questioning everyone on that appointment list as well as taking fingerprints, starting with Mrs. Pittman and Mrs. Getz, although why Mrs. Getz was examining the manuscript is a mystery to me." He winced when he realized the phrase he used. "I mean she didn't leave a sealed bid."

"She couldn't afford to bid, Jerry. She's not a wealthy woman, not like Rosemary, who, judging from the handwriting on the envelope, did leave a silent bid. Again, from the handwriting, the other silent bidder from Mystery by the Yard is Herb Jackson."

Jerry pulled a handkerchief out of his jacket pocket and mopped his face. Megan thought he looked resigned. "I suppose you looked at all the envelopes that contained the sealed bids."

It wasn't a question, but Megan answered anyway. "Of course. They were lying on the desk, so I sorted through them. Don't worry. I didn't touch them, just nudged them apart with my pencil, so I could see how many people had left bids. I happened to recognize Rosemary's and Herb's handwriting. Also, they are the only two Murder by the Yard members with enough money to bid. The rest of us just looked because that manuscript is an icon. I don't think you appreciate that, Jerry."

"I probably don't. I'm just a klutz with no culture, trying to keep some psychopath from killing the rest of you."

Megan frowned at him. It wasn't like Jerry to be so sarcastic. "That manuscript was written by a brilliant loving woman who died too young, leaving her children orphans and her husband in mourning for the rest of his life. She touched those pages, which by itself makes them precious, but she also appreciated the art of string figures, their complexity, delicacy, intricacy. She appreciated string figures as a way of communicating among people, many of whom had no written language. She was an unusual woman who preserved this particular aspect of a culture because she thought it was worth saving. Most of us don't save anything worthwhile in our lives. Oh, in case you haven't deduced this from the appointment sheet, I'm the only member of Murder by the Yard who didn't keep her date to see the manuscript. Brownleigh was already dead and the manuscript gone by the time I got here this morning, so you're wasting your time investigating me!"

"Megan, I didn't mean to insinuate that the manuscript was a piece of fluff, just that I can't see murdering anyone over it."

Megan got up and straightened her convention badge. "I can. Now if you will excuse me, I'll go in and ask Rosemary and Lorene to step out."

Holding her shoulders back and stretching her neck to get the last fraction of an inch of height, she pulled open the heavy door and slipped into the Sagebrush Room. Dr. Moser was at the podium surrounded by people, meaning the workshop was over. She searched through the crowd until she found two almost identical white curly heads, and quietly walked down the aisle and tapped Rosemary's shoulder.

"The copper wants to talk to you and Lorene."

"It was very considerate of Lieutenant Carr to wait until Dr. Moser's lecture was over," said Rosemary, "although I don't know what Lorene and I can tell him that would help. Mr. Brownleigh only showed us two pages of the manuscript, one with instructions for a Nauru Island figure and one of a variation of the Apache Door. Don't you think the story of the young Apache girl touching a door to signify what the figure was because she couldn't speak English is one of the most endearing stories in Jayne's first book? I mean we don't really know what the Apache name is, but it's always been known as the Apache Door because Jayne named it that even though all the Southwestern Indians know how to make that same figure."

She pursed her lips and looked thoughtful for a moment. "I suppose we had better also tell him that we didn't kill Mr. Brownleigh, although Reverend Wilson can certainly verify our alibis. I mean, he was the next appointment after us, and he never mentioned finding him dead."

"To be honest, Megan, our appointments were disappointing because Mr. Brownleigh showed us this box of yellowing manuscript pages," said Lorene, "but only let us examine those two, which he had laid out on that little desk. I thought he was rude because he never asked us to sit down, but he certainly made himself comfortable in that upholstered armchair, just lolled back with his hands crossed over his stomach like some kind of Oriental potentate." Megan thought Lorene's diction was endearingly anachronistic.

"He did that when I saw him, too," added Rosemary. "And frankly, he smelled just the least bit. That corduroy suit, you know. It's just too hot for corduroy in August in Texas. The whole appointment was a waste, in my opinion, but I left a sealed bid anyway. I didn't bid anything like what I can afford because I hated the thought of his making any money off me. And I didn't believe that story of his for a moment. A mother with a broken hip, indeed. You would have thought he could have come up with something better than that."

"And you saw a box full of yellowing manuscript pages, too?"

"Yes, the same box that Lorene saw."

"Were the pages that you examined written on a thick paper?"

"Yes, they were," said Lorene. "What does it mean?"

"Caroline Furness Jayne would probably have used heavyweight, thick manuscript paper of the highest grade. She could afford good paper and I don't see her not using it."

"Dr. Clark, may I have a moment of your time?" asked Dr. Moser, carefully making his way down the aisle, leaning more heavily on his cane than Megan had noticed him doing before.

"Yes, Dr. Moser, and I apologize for missing your lecture. It was one that I really wanted to hear, but I guess I'll have to be happy with an audiotape. Given the circumstances and all, I couldn't get away."

"Hmm, yes, murder does seem to be a distraction. But, my dear, I'll tell you anything you want to know about Mrs. Jayne, so don't worry that you missed my formal lecture." He leaned over and whispered in her ear. "To be honest, my dear, my informal lectures are much better. But excuse me, I didn't mean to interrupt your conversation with these lovely ladies." He bowed to Rosemary and Lorene, and Megan swore they twittered. She thought twittering only occurred in Southern novels.

"You're not interrupting, Dr. Moser. I was telling Rosemary and Lorene that Lieutenant Carr is waiting to take their statements. He's taking statements in the ~~der of appointments, so you would be number ~~ Megan. "By the way, why did you sign up for two appointments, the one at nine forty-five last night, and the one at nine this morning?"

Dr. Moser looked down at the floor and drew circles on the carpet with his cane. Finally, he raised his head. "I'm embarrassed to admit it, Dr. Clark, but I was hoping I could persuade him to open the bids and allow me to top the highest. It was a very unethical move on my part, and I'm ashamed of myself. But what shames me even more is that the only thing that stopped me from committing a dishonorable act was murder. If someone had not murdered Clyde Brownleigh, I would have nefariously won the bidding as surely as I'm standing here."

"Are you planning to tell Lieutenant Carr about your intentions?" asked Megan.

"I feel that I would exonerate myself by doing so."

"I wouldn't if I were you," said Megan. "Lieutenant Carr's profession requires a literal mind, and he might, *might*, misinterpret your effort at self-exoneration for a confession. Isn't that right, Rosemary, Lorene?"

"Absolutely," said Rosemary. "I wouldn't add to Lieutenant Carr's confusion. After all, you may be the only one who has an alibi. Clyde Brownleigh had been dead for quite some time when you opened his door this morning."

"No, that's not true, Rosemary," said Megan. "Actually, none of us has an alibi. Any of us could have knocked on his door after the appointments were done."

"Personally, I think poison is more Lorene's and

my forte," said Rosemary, patting Megan's cheek as she and the other member of the duo Megan called "the Twins" marched down the aisle toward the door and Lieutenant Carr.

Megan hated having her cheek patted. And she hoped that Rosemary and Lorene had better sense than to mention poison. Jerry did have such a literal mind.

10

It is impossible ... not to make inferences; the mistake is to depend on them. ... In detection one should take no chances, give no one the benefit of the doubt.

—REEVES in Ronald A. Knox's
The Viaduct Murder, 1925

The High Plains Motel's meeting rooms are situated in an L-shaped block on one side of the rectangle that constitutes the business office, bar, kitchen facilities—in other words, the nuts and bolts of motel management. Otherwise, the motel is built around an open square, with swimming pool, hot tub, restaurant, and foliage of all kinds and sizes within its hollow center. The door to the Sagebrush Room happens to be on the short end of the L with a good view of the open area, and nearly directly across from the so-called Apache Door Hospitality Room. The only areas I couldn't see were the registration desk and the bar, but Special Crimes had already searched there and found nothing, just as Megan predicted. I wasn't sure why she was so certain that the manuscript would not be found, considering that unless a member of Murder by the Yard sent Brownleigh to his just reward, all the other convention attendees were strangers to the area, and most had flown into Amarillo rather than driven. For those of you who live on the East Coast, where you can drive to four states in an afternoon, let me inform you that the West is a huge amount of empty space dotted by a few overpopulated metroplexes, such as Denver, Dallas–Fort Worth, Phoenix, Los Angeles, San Francisco, and Houston. Texas alone takes more than a day to drive across. My point is that few attendees had cars in which to either hide a manuscript or transport it to another location for hiding. And only an idiot would call a cab, and I hadn't noticed any idiots registered at this convention, at least so far as IQ is concerned. So where was the blasted box of yellowing pages?

I didn't have a clue.

Judging from how much tighter the skin was stretched over Jerry Carr's skull each time he walked by my chair, he didn't have a clue, either. He was one of those individuals whose skin draws up with worry rather than going slack and folding into more furrows than a newly plowed wheatfield. Much more lack of progress in the investigation and the skin on his face was liable to split down the middle.

I maintained my post outside the door of the Sagebrush Room, leisurely changing signs as each new workshop began, a less than onerous task that allowed me to observe Jerry Carr's Special Crimes Unit escorting those whose names were on the appointment sheet to the Yucca Room next door. It was the only meeting room which had four solid

walls instead of those leather-looking panels on
each side that will fold like an accordion to make
two or three or four rooms into one megaspace for
a banquet or for a speaker more than fifty people
might want to hear. Either Jerry and his Special
Crimes henchman, as well as whoever was giving a
statement, spoke in quiet, civilized tones, or the
walls of the Yucca Room were also soundproofed,
because I couldn't hear a thing. Except when Jerry
interviewed Denise LeClerc. Her, I heard. She had
one of those voices that was not only high-pitched
but loud, so the listener had the worst of auditory
possibilities.

"I demand to give my statement next, Lieutenant.
There is a very interesting paper to be given in the
next workshop, plus I will be demonstrating several
string figures immediately afterward, and I *would*
not care to be dragged out by the Gestapo in the
middle of either the paper or my demonstration just
to answer asinine questions."

"Mumble, mumble, mumble." Jerry's question was
inaudible, so I had to guess what he asked by Denise's answer, which was audible to anyone standing
outside the door, or outside in the parking lot, for all
· I knew.

"I *know* I was the last person with an appointment
to see Clyde Brownleigh last night. You don't have
to tell me what I did or did not do. He was alive in
all his disgusting, mercenary piggish glory when I
left him, so don't insinuate in any way that I might
have strangled him! What I might have *wished* to do

to him is another matter, but wishes are not indictable offenses; at least they weren't in the late sixties when I was more politically active than I am now."

"Mumble, mumble, mumble." Jerry Carr asked his next question, which again I could only guess at by listening to Denise's answer.

"Of course I do. Lieutenant, I would vouch that *everyone* attending this convention knows how to do Cheating the Hangman, that one and A Hand Catch, which is another trick figure."

"Mumble, mumble, mumble." Another question from Jerry. I wished he spoke at least half as loud as Denise.

"Yes, I left a bid. Why would I make an appointment otherwise? Not for the privilege of his company! I would rather spend time with a skunk!"

"Mumble, mumble, mumble."

"Just to see the manuscript? You mean others made appointments just to look at the page or two Brownleigh allowed us to study? Then I would be very suspicious of those particular people, Lieutenant, because they had a motive to strangle that little jerk. They wanted the manuscript, didn't have the money to buy it, so one or the other or maybe all of them together killed him for it. I hope you are searching the homes of our hosts and hostesses, because in my opinion, one or more of them is guilty."

"Mumble, mumble, mumble."

"Did I see anyone entering Brownleigh's room after I left? Why, Lieutenant, are you asking me to rat out my associates?"

"Mumble, mumble, material witness, mumble." Jerry's voice was getting louder, enough so that I could catch a word or two.

"Don't threaten to jail me as a material witness, Lieutenant. You have not an iota of proof that I saw anyone or heard anything."

"Mumble, whereabouts between twelve and four, mumble." Jerry's voice kept rising, so his patience must be somewhere between slim and none.

"I took a swim after my appointment, then went to my room. But I'm not the one you should be asking to explain her whereabouts. After all, I wasn't the one sneaking out of Brownleigh's room at one o'clock."

"WHO IN THE DEVIL DID YOU SEE?" When Jerry decided to raise his voice, he did so with a vengeance.

I leaned closer to the door and fell out of my chair, banging my head on the doorknob in the process. But I heard every word Denise LeClerc said.

"Dr. Stevens, are you all right? May I call a doctor for you? That's an awful-looking bump on your head." Dr. Moser knelt down beside me and pressed a pristine white handkerchief against my forehead.

I grabbed his wrist and nearly toppled the old man over. "Did you hear what Denise said?"

Dr. Moser freed his wrist and managed to pull himself to his feet by using his cane as leverage, an alarmed expression on his face. I suppose I did look maniacal when I grabbed him, so I can't blame him for backing away a step or two. I pushed myself into a sitting position and decided to wait until my head stopped whirling around before making any further moves.

Finally, Dr. Moser spoke. "I'm afraid my hearing is not as acute as yours, but I wouldn't take seriously anything that Denise LeClerc says. She is a trouble-maker who enjoys creating a fuss."

Dr. Moser was the only person I had ever heard actually use the word "fuss." It was an old-fashioned word that described the end result of Denise Le-Clerc's meddling with no further adjectives needed.

"So you didn't hear her mention a name?"

"No, I'm sorry, I didn't. But I'm sure we will know soon enough whom Denise has accused."

I already knew.

Megan was sitting on the aisle seat in the first row of chairs in the Sagebrush Room, waiting her turn to give a formal statement and in the meantime madly writing down instructions for every string figure demonstrated, using her simplified nomenclature. Randal claims that only an idiot could fail to follow Megan's nomenclature.

Such broadly condemnatory statements are one of the reasons I'm not Randal Anderson's best buddy. I would never condemn those with a poor sense of spacial relations.

I knelt down by her chair and whispered in her ear. "We've got trouble right here in River City and it's spelled Denise. Actually, it's not Denise, it's whoever she saw at Brownleigh's door last night at one o'clock. You wouldn't know who that was, would you?"

"Your forehead is bleeding."

"I *know* I'm bleeding. Did you hear what I said?"

Megan closed her notebook, picked up her backpack, and jerked her head toward the door. "Let's go. I want to know exactly how you found out whatever it is you're talking about."

As soon as we were outside the Sagebrush Room, I grasped her arm and aimed her toward a tree growing in an enormous pot a few feet away. I wasn't hiding her—exactly—but I did shift her around so the tree was between her and the door to the Yucca Room. As short as she was, the large clay pot was nearly taller than she. Then I told her verbatim everything that I had overheard. She sighed.

"I expected more of a reaction than a sigh," I said. "I expected at least assault and battery on the person of Denise LeClerc. You've been unjustly accused! Don't you have anything to say for yourself?"

"If you're going to be an eavesdropper, Ryan, I wish you would learn to do a better job. You should have listened to what all the witnesses said. As it is, we don't know any more than we did before. Everybody knows how to construct Cheating the Hangman. Even the members of Murder by the Yard know. We all have been in Brownleigh's room, so fingerprint evidence is worthless. We all want the manuscript, and we all have means, motive, and opportunity. But now we apparently have a witness: Denise LeClerc.

I wonder what she was doing lurking around Brownleigh's room?"

"She was swimming, Megan! What I want to know is what you were doing?"

Megan wrinkled her forehead, an unconscious habit her mother claimed would age her prematurely. "Denise LeClerc doesn't strike me as the type to go swimming at midnight."

Megan brings new meaning to the phrase "driving one to drink." I would have been an alcoholic for the past year if I weren't allergic to brewer's yeast.

"Damn it, Megan, did you go see Clyde Brownleigh last night?"

Her expression was more indignant than guilty. In fact, it was mostly indignant, as if my questions invaded her privacy. "Yes, but it wasn't one o'clock. It was closer to twelve-thirty. I wonder why Denise specifically said one o'clock." Megan nibbled her thumbnail, another habit her mother abhors, and looked thoughtful.

I, on the other hand, probably looked appalled. "Megan! Listen to me! It doesn't make a hill of beans difference if it's one o'clock or twelve-thirty. The fact is you drove back to the motel and sneaked into Brownleigh's room."

"Of course it makes a difference. If baseball is a game of inches, then crime solving is a game of minutes. I'm really curious about those thirty minutes."

Rearing all four of my children to adulthood failed to give me the same number of gray hairs that Megan Clark has added to my head in the past year. "I don't think Lieutenant Carr will split hairs over a thirty-minute discrepancy—plus you weren't honest with him. You told him that you didn't see Brownleigh and the manuscript."

"No, what I told Jerry was that I hadn't kept my appointment because Brownleigh was dead, and that I hadn't seen the manuscript. Both those statements are true. My appointment was for nine-thirty this morning—when Brownleigh was rather obviously dead—and I never saw the manuscript. Brownleigh refused to show me anything except the box in which he kept it. I was breaking his rules. I suspect that if I had waved a million dollars in front of those greedy little eyes, he would have given me that manuscript as fast as he could get it out of the box. But I didn't have a million dollars, and he knew it. And I turned down his other proposition."

"You mean he tried to seduce you?"

Now she had a disbelieving expression on her face. "Ryan! In order to seduce, you must be seductive, and that little toad was *not* seductive. Plus, he smelled like damp corduroy. He made a nasty verbal pass, followed by an attempted grope, and I kicked him in what is probably his most beloved area, and walked out. I did *not sneak,* and I saw no one in the hall, which makes me wonder if dear Dr. LeClerc was even lurking near, or if she imagined this scenario for some purpose of her own."

"And she just happened to guess right, is that what you're telling me? Megan, this is not some complex string figure that you're unraveling to see how it's constructed, this is a murder investigation, and you're it! It doesn't matter if LeClerc made a lucky guess or actually saw you, Jerry Carr is going to come roaring out of the Yucca Room after your carcass, and you had better have Call Me Herb on call—so to speak."

"Megan!" It was Jerry Carr and he sounded as if he knew exactly where Megan was—which he probably did, since all he had to do was look for the red hair, and he couldn't miss that curly head just visible over the top of that giant clay pot.

"Damn!" exclaimed Megan in what was for her an infrequent use of minor profanity. Not that she used major profanity; she didn't curse at all. She considered obscene language the sign of an inadequate vocabulary.

"If I didn't have this convention to worry about, I would manage to be 'unavailable' until I could solve this murder, but I suppose I can't do that under the circumstances," said Megan, in as resigned a tone of voice as I've ever heard her use.

"Thank God, you're not going to be playing sleuth for this murder. Your last sleuthing aged me ten years. This time let Jerry Carr and his cops handle it. He knows you're not guilty of strangling the toad—I mean, Brownleigh."

Megan stepped around the clay pot into plain view of the head of Special Crimes. She waved her hand—hardly necessary, since there couldn't be more than twenty feet between her and Jerry Carr. "Jerry, I'm over here! Do you need me for something?"

"You might say that," said Jerry, walking toward us.

Megan turned to me and smiled. "I didn't mean I wasn't planning to solve this murder, Ryan. I only meant that I can't be 'unavailable' while I do it."

I opened my mouth to chide her—actually to lecture her on the dangers of being stupid—when the screaming started. I turned around in time to see Candi Hobbs staggering out of the Sagebrush Room holding a yellowing piece of manuscript between two fingers like she had found something nasty and was looking for a wastebasket. I heard Megan mutter, "Oh, my God," as she ran toward Candi, who was being supported by a very frightened-looking Randal Anderson.

"Ryan, find Herb Jackson—fast!" hollered Megan over her shoulder as she beat Jerry Carr to Candi by a step.

11

A WINKING EYE

A Hawaiian figure from the island of Kauai.

1. Insert L2 and L3 (Left Index Finger and Left Middle Finger) into a loop of string and let it hang loose.

2. Grasp the Far String of the loop, and bring it toward you completely wrapping it around L2 and L3 (Left Index Finger and Left Middle Finger).

3. Grasp the Far String and place it between L1 and L2 (Left Thumb and Left Index Finger) and release the string.

4. Insert 1 (Left Thumb) under the string that wraps around L2 and L3 (Left Index Finger and Left Middle Finger).

5. Bring the long string hanging around L1 and L2 (Left Thumb and Left Index Finger) back over L1 (Left Thumb) and release it.

6. Grasp the Far Hanging String and place it between L1 and L2 and release string.

7. Grasp the Two Hanging Strings, and pull them, make the eye wink.

"You have the right to remain silent . . ."

Megan held out her hand. "Hand me the piece of paper, Jerry, and I'll sign it. There's no point in wasting time reading me my rights. I can read them for myself, and besides, I'm familiar with the Miranda warning from your faux pas last spring."

"I wouldn't call my reading the Miranda to you a social blunder," replied Jerry Carr, sitting across from her at a banquet table in the Yucca Room, tape recorder and video recorder at the ready, with a couple of telephones provided by the motel. It was a mini–crime room, but it would do.

"Sorry, wrong term."

"It is unless you consider that I haven't even been able to talk you into going out with me for something as innocent as a cup of coffee since then. How long are you going to punish me for doing my job?"

Megan felt her face grow hot and knew she was turning a lovely shade of tomato red. She had been avoiding Jerry for no other reason than her belief that loyalty was the greatest of virtues, and Jerry put the law ahead of loyalty to her. That marked him as an honorable, ethical man, dedicated to Justice with a capital *J,* and she ought to be ashamed of herself. And when she had time, she would. But for now she felt the cold shadow of prison threatening her, and she wasn't interested in Jerry's honorable behavior as much as she was in his investigative skills, and those seemed to be focused on her and Candi, but mostly on her, instead of on tracking whoever strangled that little toad Clyde Brownleigh.

"It's difficult to stay friends with someone who is always one day away from arresting you."

Jerry tapped his pencil on the table, took several deep breaths, and began talking in what Megan considered a quiet reasonable voice. "And whose fault is that? Damn it, Megan, you're always sticking your nose where it doesn't belong. You discover murder victims. Do you have any idea how many murder victims are 'discovered' by their murderers? A truckload, that's how many. Then you don't faint or run away screaming like the normal woman would, you squat down and do a quick once-over on the corpse, check out the crime scene before my techs even show up, and have a damn theory ready for me when I walk through the door. Logically, what am I supposed to think?"

Megan winced as Jerry's voice rose to a shout. "You are supposed to believe me."

"Believe you! If my mother hadn't threatened to disown me if I ever arrested 'that cute little librarian,' you would already be very familiar with the inside of the Potter County Correctional Center. I've cut you more slack than any suspect I've ever dealt with, Megan."

"I'm sorry, Jerry, but did it ever occur to you that you might be able to use my skills instead of immediately yelling 'interference' whenever I make a suggestion?"

Jerry ran his fingers through his hair, leaned back in his chair, and studied the ceiling much like Megan noticed Ryan doing just before delivering a lecture aimed at improving her attitude or behavior. "Megan, the criminal-justice system has procedures which every law-enforcement officer has to follow. You bypass or trample all those procedures, putting yourself and the community in danger, and risk letting a criminal go free because the crime scene has been contaminated by a civilian rooting through the evidence."

"And if you had listened to me last spring, you would have caught the murderer instead of me. But you thought my theory was silly, so I was forced to prove it. And I don't 'root' through evidence. I'm very careful."

Jerry sighed. "Can we skip the recriminations left over from the last case and get to this one."

"I don't know about you, but that's why I'm here. Otherwise, I would be listening to Reverend Wilson's workshop on the Nauru Island repertoire," said Megan.

"Were you in Clyde Brownleigh's room last night at one o'clock?"

"No."

"Megan, I have a signed statement from a witness who saw you leaving his room at one A.M."

"Denise LeClerc is lying. I left Brownleigh's room around twelve-thirty and he was still alive and the autopsy will prove it, so if she saw someone leaving at one, it wasn't me."

Jerry Carr looked surprised for a brief moment before he assumed what Megan called his "official mask." "How did you know that Denise—" he began before his mouth snapped closed.

"She has a loud voice," replied Megan.

"Your good friend Dr. Stevens, I suppose," said Jerry in a resigned voice.

Megan thought the answer so self-evident that she didn't bother to say anything.

"How will the autopsy prove you were in his room and he was still alive at twelve-thirty?"

"Certain bruising which could only have occurred before death. The pathologist will be able to estimate how long before death the bruising occurred with some degree of accuracy, enough to cast doubt on Denise's statement that it was me who left Brownleigh's room at one. I believe that Brownleigh was killed somewhere around one or shortly after, and once the pathologist finds the bruising, no jury will believe that anyone as small as I in comparison to the victim would have stayed in that room once she kicked him where I did."

"You kicked Brownleigh in the nu—" Jerry snapped off the word in mid-syllable and covered his face with his hands, but Megan could hear his smothered laughter anyway, and felt better about Jerry Carr.

"It's my usual response to a slimy proposition, and it's much faster than suing for sexual harassment."

"Dr. Clark," said Jerry, dabbing at his eyes with a handkerchief, "please remain at your current address, because I will want to talk to you again after the autopsy results are in."

Megan got up and hooked her backpack in one hand up from where it rested on the floor. "I'll be at home, where I've been for the past year. I think I'll claim my right to a lawyer if there's another interview, Jerry. Herb Jackson is representing Candi, so I suppose I'll have Mother call one of her lawyer cronies from her days fighting the Department of Energy over the nuclear-waste dump. I think I want the short guy who gave such wonderful interviews. Just imagine what he could do with a curly redheaded librarian as a client."

"Oh, God, he's worse than listening to Herb Jackson for two hours." The lieutenant of Special Crimes folded his arms on the top of the banquet table and laid his head down. "Get out of here, Megan," he ordered in a muffled voice.

Most of the lights were off in Time and Again Bookstore, and Agnes had hung posters over the store's one front window so no curious passerby could look in and see the entire membership of the Murder by the Yard Reading Circle having a literary discussion at midnight. The store was filled with shadows, with the only lights being one over the checkout counter and the one over the reading area, where the membership sat closer to one another than usual. The faint sounds of live music from the tiny dance clubs and restaurants down the street, the scent of Oriental spices (Agnes believed in potpourri), the creaks of the old building, and the whine of a strong wind blowing outside added to the eerie atmosphere of the meeting, whose subject was murder.

"I didn't steal the manuscript, Megan," said a tearful Candi Hobbs as she sat on the couch in Time and Again Bookstore's reading area. "But without Herb Jackson's intervention, I'm sure I would be spending tonight in jail. Thank you so much, Herb." Herb straightened his vest and preened as much as he was able, Herb not being a natural preener.

Randal Anderson hovered to Candi's right, while the Twins, Rosemary and Lorene, hovered to her left. Randal's idea of comfort consisted of pats on Candi's shoulder and assurances that "everything would be all right." Rosemary and Lorene plied her with cups of hot tea and generous helpings of their homemade chocolate-chip and coconut-macaroon cookies. Megan thought that many more cookies and Candi would gain back all the weight she had lost over the summer. In the interests of Candi's retaining her new svelte figure, as well as assuring at least one cookie apiece for the rest of the membership of Murder by the Yard, Megan decided it was time to take up the gavel and open this meeting.

"I believe you, Candi, but can you tell us where you found one of the missing manuscript pages?"

Candi sniffed and dabbed her eyes. "It was in my purse, this one here." She gestured to a large, square black bag that reminded Megan of the purses her mother carried, but her mother always needed the space for spray paint, rolls of paper for banners, and petitions for whatever cause she was currently supporting. Megan couldn't imagine what Candi carried in hers.

"I always carry extra notebooks and I had my copy of Caroline Furness Jayne's book and several other volumes on string figures, as well as all my loops, and there it was—tucked between the pages of *String Figures and How to Make Them.* I couldn't have been more scared if there had been a snake in my purse. I was just so shocked," continued Candi, alternating talking and sipping hot tea and nibbling chocolate-chip cookies.

"Okay, so someone slipped a page of the missing manuscript in your purse. Who had access to it—other than Randal?" asked Megan.

Randal sat up in a huff. "I beg your pardon. I do *not* mess around in ladies' purses, particularly not Candi's, without permission, and I certainly did not kill Clyde Brownleigh and steal the manuscript. Even if I did, why would I want to throw suspicion on Candi, whom I happen to be fond of?"

"Oh, Randal!" said Candi in a breathy voice that Megan wasn't aware the girl possessed.

Randal blushed, a phenomenon almost equal in unlikelihood as his revealing a sense of humor during the reading group's last murder investigation. If murder victims kept turning up at regular intervals, Megan thought Randal had a better-than-average chance of becoming likable.

"Well, it's true," said Randal, blushing an even darker red.

"If we can skip the romantic confessions for the

present, you haven't answered my question, Candi. Who besides Randal had an opportunity to slip a manuscript page into your purse? Furthermore, who would want to? Who would want to cast suspicion on Candi, and why? Candi, what can you tell us?" asked Megan.

Candi nibbled on a coconut macaroon as she thought. Watching her reminded Megan that she hadn't eaten since a hurried lunch between workshops.

"I'm not sure, Megan. I always carry my purse with me and set it on the floor beside my chair. And Randal always sits by me." Candi smiled at Randal as though he were king of the world.

"Who sat on your other side, Candi?" said Megan. "You have more than one."

"Oh, yes, well, let me think." Candi pursed her lips and screwed up her eyes in what was her usual thoughtful expression. "Rosemary and Lorene sit by me most of the time, and Herb does sometimes. Agnes hardly ever does because she has to watch her book booth."

"But we didn't this afternoon," said Rosemary, her denial accompanied by Lorene's nod of agreement. "We had to each give statements to Lieutenant Carr, so when we both finished and finally got to the workshop, all the seats were taken on your row. Let me think, who was sitting next to you?"

"I remember now!" exclaimed Candi. "It was that horrible LeClerc woman, the one I poured the pitcher of water on."

"How could you forget Denise sitting by you?" asked Megan, astonished by Candi's obtuseness. If Megan had been mad enough to dump an entire pitcher of ice water over someone's head, she would still be holding a grudge, and would certainly be aware of that person sitting next to her.

"I was concentrating on Mark Sherman's lecture on three-dimensional string figures—it was so fascinating—and didn't pay much attention to her. Besides, I don't hold grudges. I have completely forgotten her impolite statements of this morning," said Candi.

"That's such a Christian attitude," said Lorene.

"It certainly is," agreed Rosemary, patting Candi's cheek.

"Actually, it's not Candi's Christian actions that should concern us," said Megan, feeling frustrated at how often people missed the point. "It's Denise LeClerc's lack of forgiveness that has landed both Candi and me in Jerry Carr's soup."

"You mean Denise may have slipped that manuscript page into my purse?" asked Candi, with a surprised expression that Megan would swear was genuine.

"When you think about it objectively, Denise may have been feeling a little hostile over this morning's pitcher incident," said Ryan in his first contribution to the conversation since his diatribe to Megan about having a meeting of the reading circle to discuss the murder in the first place.

"Thinking objectively, what's her excuse to add me to her hit list?" asked Megan.

"Other than jealousy because you're younger and prettier, I imagine it was because you witnessed her humiliation and didn't reprimand Candi," answered Ryan.

"But we all witnessed her humiliation," said Agnes, bookstore owner and, in Megan's opinion, one of the more sensible members of Murder by the Yard.

"Then we might all be prepared to be fingered." Ryan smiled as if proud of himself. He glanced around the circle in growing bewilderment to find all the members staring at him with expressions varying from pity to puzzlement. "Isn't 'fingered' the right expression?" he whispered to Megan.

"You've been watching old George Raft movies on cable again, haven't you?" asked Megan, thinking that Ryan was absolutely hopeless when it came to understanding the world of mysteries.

"How did you know?"

"Because 'fingered' is a word that hasn't been commonly used in any decently written mystery for about fifty years." Megan raised her voice. "Ryan makes a valid point. I think we're all at risk for some form of revenge from Denise."

"What did she do to you, Megan?" Agnes asked in an apologetic tone. "Sitting at my booth all day—except for my visit with Jerry Carr—has left me out of the loop. I was the last one to hear about poor Candi."

"I'm a suspect along with Candi. We've been read

our rights, and the only reason we're not in jail wait-ing to be bonded out is because Jerry knows we didn't murder anybody, no matter how bad it looks. Besides, he has to have some evidence to support Denise's claims, and he doesn't have it."

"Not claims—lies," said Randal Anderson.

"Claims is the right word, Randal," said Megan. "The manuscript page was found on Candi, and I did go see Clyde Brownleigh last night after all the ap-pointments were over. But what is interesting is the one lie Denise did tell." She explained the thirty-minute difference between the time of her actions and Denise's account.

Rosemary nodded her head like a wise woman in the Peruvian village high in the Andes where Megan spent three months doing a research project for her master's program in anthropology. "I agree with you, Megan. We need to investigate what Denise was do-ing near Brownleigh's room, and what she did in that missing thirty minutes."

"You can't do that!" Ryan looked as desperate as he did in his truck on the way to the bookstore when he and Megan had had this same argument.

"You don't need to shout," said Megan. "And if you're going to give me the same lecture you did both last spring and an hour ago about interfering in a police investigation, don't bother. As I see it, Candi and I need to be proactive in this situation. After all, we're the ones who might end up working in the prison library."

"You certainly will if you interfere!" shouted

Ryan, kicking his chair over in his effort to rise. "I'm warning you, Megan, sooner or later Jerry Carr is going to run out of patience with you."

"I hope it's later. I don't have time to bother with Jerry Carr. Now, back to the subject of LeClerc. Who's going to become her confidant and learn whom she did see at one o'clock?" asked Megan. "It can't be Candi or Randal, since the Lady LeClerc is displeased with both of them. And Herb is Candi's lawyer, so I don't think he can do it. Rosemary, Lorene, what about you?"

Lorene and Rosemary looked at each other, then at Megan. They both shook their heads no at the same time.

"I'm afraid I can't, Megan," said Rosemary. "I gave that young woman a piece of my mind this morning for the way she talked about Candi. I just walked right up to her outside the Sagebrush Room before Dr. Moser gave his wonderful lecture on Caroline Furness Jayne, and I told her how ashamed her mother would be if she had heard how her daughter talked."

"What did she say?" asked Megan, who would have bet Denise LeClerc sprang from a toadstool spore rather than a woman's womb.

"She said her mother was who taught her to, uh, speak her mind." Rosemary leaned closer to Megan and lowered her voice. "Speak her mind wasn't actually what she said, but I don't want to dirty my mouth by repeating her. All I can say is that her people must be poor quality to raise two generations of such trashy women, and I don't care if Denise LeClerc is well educated or not. Education doesn't always overcome upbringing."

Megan nodded. "I see your point. I doubt Denise would overlook your recent conversation with her." She turned to Lorene. "Did you chastise the Lady LeClerc, too?"

"I told her she must be an unhappy maladjusted person to treat Candi and Randal the way she did," said Lorene, handing Candi another coconut macaroon. "Have another sip of tea, dear, and you'll feel better."

"What did she say?" asked Megan.

"I'm afraid she told me to go to hell. I'll admit that I was a little judgmental, but consigning one to hell is serious business. I forgave her, of course, but it was hard."

Feeling a little desperate, Megan turned to Agnes. "We'll all take turns watching your booth if you'll take on LeClerc."

Agnes was a gnome-sized woman with silky brown hair tucked neatly into a knot at the back of her head, and hooded blue eyes that could be kindly or icy, depending on whether someone was on her good side or bad side. She wore brown support hose under her slacks, sensible shoes with crepe soles, and a sweater winter and summer. She was also a spinster. "Too late to look for a man now," she had once told Megan. "The good ones are taken, and the others are Viagra-dependent. If I get lonely, I'll get one of those little dogs, the yapping kind, to keep me company. They don't get mad if you open up a can for supper."

She had lived in the little apartment in back of the bookstore all her life, which made her one of Sixth Street's oldest continuous residents. Originally, Sixth Street had been Route 66, and a flourishing business district with prosperous homes on the side streets. When I-40 was built, and business fell off, Agnes stayed, barely making a living from her used-book store. "I'm just like those Okies who used to drive down Sixth Street when it was Route 66. They were looking for better times and so was I. Now Sixth Street is a national historical monument, and there are more antique stores and fancy little restaurants and clubs than you can shake a stick at. Just goes to show what faith will do. I had faith that Sixth Street would rise again, and it did."

"Agnes," repeated Megan, feeling a little desperate.

"I'm sorry, Megan, but I gave that young woman— and by the way, she's not as young as she would like you to believe—a talking-to and refused her business. There is no good reason to be as tacky as she is, and I don't need money badly enough to take hers."

"Bravo, Agnes!" cried Randal, interrupting his hovering enough to applaud. "Principle over profit! What a gal!"

"That's wonderful, Agnes," said the Twins in a chorus.

"Somebody has to be her confidant," shouted Megan so she would be heard over the standing ovation. "If we can't talk to her, we'll never know who else she saw coming out of Brownleigh's room last night, and Candi and I will be suspects forever—because that's how long it will take Jerry Carr to solve this crime without our help."

"Excuse me, Megan," said Rosemary. "But I believe Denise LeClerc did have a good word to say about Ryan."

12

THE MOON GONE DARK

A continuation of a figure called the Moon, from the Mwezi, in Central Africa, but also found in Torres Straits, Andaman Island, and the Caroline Islands. The continuation which is the Moon Gone Dark is found among the Mwakatanga in Central Africa.

First Figure: The Moon

1. Opening A.

2. Take 5f (Right and Left Little Finger Far String) in the mouth, and bring over the other loops, at the same time releasing 5 (Right and Left Little Fingers), but don't extend.

3. Transfer 1 Loops (Right and Left Thumb Loops) to 5 (Right and Left Little Fingers), and insert 2 (Right and Left Index Fingers) into the Mouth Loop from below.

4. Extend and let go of Mouth Loop.

5. Navajo 2 Loops (Bring Lower Loop on Right and Left Index Fingers over the Upper Loop and off each finger). Extend.

I don't know why I let Megan talk me into projects like this. Did I say projects? That's the wrong word. Disaster, catastrophe, even Armageddon are more accurate nouns to describe any activity that Megan Clark plans. Sitting on a couch next to Dr. Denise LeClerc in the Apache Door Hospitality Room at ten o'clock in the morning was not to be endured sober. Unfortunately, I was. Sober, that is. So was Denise, and what is worse, she was wearing both perfume and makeup. I wouldn't have noticed if Megan hadn't told me. Except the perfume. I've always liked light, flowery scents on a woman, as if she had just come in from some garden wearing some kind of floaty long dress and straw hat tied on with a scarf, with an armful of roses and peach blossoms and violets and lilac. Denise went for the heavier musk scents that always remind me of large mammals in heat. I could imagine a Brahma bull pawing the ground and snorting at a delicate young cow. I'm certain that's not the image that Denise sought to project.

"So tell me about your minicourse on Custer's Last Stand," Denise purred.

In the first place I don't like the Battle of the Little Big Horn referred to as Custer's Last Stand. It was the single-most-spectacular defeat of the Indian Wars, and the worst massacre of U.S. soldiers. It was a tragedy that is still debated today with just as much fierce passion as it was in 1876 when it occurred. Should Custer have attacked the Sioux and Cheyenne village without waiting for other columns to arrive? Should Custer have split his command? Did his men panic when faced with overwhelming numbers? There are enough legitimate issues about the Battle of the Little Big Horn to fuel a month-long debate, which would probably disintegrate into a physical brawl within a week. That's how passionate those inflicted with Custermania are, regardless of whether they are for or against George Armstrong Custer. To call it Custer's Last Stand reduces the battle to the level of a B-movie Western.

In the second place, I don't like woman who purr—or attempt to—and run their fingers up the crease of my pants—especially when I'm wearing Levi's and don't have a crease. I kept moving away, crossing my legs to take the imaginary crease out of range, and otherwise discourage Denise. But the woman was as tenacious as a sand flea: she just burrowed in and stayed. Finally, I got up and walked around—which didn't help much because she followed me, patting my arm and attempting to rub my back until I stood plastered against a wall. I haven't been groped that much since I was sixteen and in the backseat of my daddy's old Ford Fairlane with Donna Sue Grady, possessor of the largest breasts in the junior class of my high school.

Her groping I didn't mind.

Denise LeClerc was, in the vernacular, another kettle of fish.

"It's not a minicourse," I finally said. "It's a series of public lectures in which students may receive credit if they submit a paper. I think of it as more of a graduate-level seminar that is open to the public.

The response has been good, so I suppose I shall continue until I'm lecturing to an empty auditorium."

"So what is your emphasis in your lectures? Custer, the vainglorious stud whose ego killed his command, or Custer the hero, fighting to the last man?" Denise fluttered her eyelashes, a less than attractive sight.

"Neither one. Custer was actually following standard military procedure when he split his command and ordered Reno to ride through the village, chasing the Sioux and Cheyenne into Custer's waiting arms. That was usually the way it was done: ride through a village and chase the Indians out the other end without their tipis, horses, and other possessions. In Custer's case, he underestimated the numbers of Sioux and Cheyenne, and overestimated the grit of Major Reno, who mucked up his part of the whole attack. Custer a hero? According to the accounts of the winners of the battle, the Seventh Calvary died well. If that's the measure of a hero, then I guess Custer and his men were heroes." I smiled and sat down in one of the overstuffed chairs, a safe way to avoid sitting by Denise.

Denise plopped down on the arm of my chair, and I lurched up and across the room to the door, through which Dr. Moser and several of the other string-figure enthusiasts had barely entered. "Dr. Moser, it's good to see you. I hope you had a good night's sleep. Did you just get out of String Tricks and Catches? I wanted to make that one, but the responsibilities of being a host have kept me on the run. Denise and I were just talking about how much we were looking forward to the workshop on the Arctic String-Figure Project." I didn't mention that I would be outside of the Sagebrush Room ready to change signs, while Denise would be *inside* the room with a door between us. I would lock the door to maintain such a status quo, but I doubt the fire department would approve of my violating their fire safety code.

Denise oozed over to my side. "No, we weren't, Ryan dear. We were talking about Custer and the Last Stand."

Ryan dear? My God, but Megan will owe me for this one.

"Fascinating man, General Custer," said Dr. Moser. "A far stretch from string figures as a subject for conversation, but I don't blame you for not wanting to discuss the convention."

"Why is that, Dr. Moser?" asked Megan, who was making faces at me behind Denise's back. I think she wanted to learn about my progress as a spy. I made faces back, all threatening physical violence, beginning with scalping—the technicalities of which I have known all my professional career, but have always lacked a subject upon which to practice.

Dr. Moser sat down on the couch and carefully laid his cane on the floor out of the way. He took a sip of water, cast me a sympathetic look, and replied to Megan in a low, somber voice. "We, and I think I speak for my colleagues, looked forward to this convention. The proposed workshops sounded interesting, and the papers to be presented during some of them promised to break new ground in the under-standing of how string figures function in a culture. And I am still interested in the papers and workshops. But the camaraderie is gone, burned up in the flames of suspicion."

Dr. Moser had a nice sense of figurative language, but Megan was focused on the factual. "What exactly do you mean, Dr. Moser?" she asked.

The elderly mathematician took another sip of wa-ter. "It's the murder. Not exactly what you expect as a highlight of a convention, but unfortunately, it is what we received. It's not that we all liked Brown-leigh, because most of us didn't, and if we were all truthful, it's the missing manuscript that we grieve for more than him. Perhaps that says something about us as human beings—or perhaps it says something about him. But that missing manuscript is what has spoiled the civility of the convention. We all look at one another and wonder. 'Did you do it?' we want to ask. 'Did you steal Caroline Furness Jayne's most precious work?' "

Dr. Yahara came forward from the back of the room. He was such a polite man, with the reserve that we Americans stereotype as typically Oriental, that I had not noticed him much during the conven-tion. When he began to speak, he had my attention as well as that of every other person in the room. Even Denise stopped pawing me.

"As you know, I am the foremost string figure en-thusiast in Japan, and I have, in your words, my heart set on the lost Jayne manuscript. I made a bid for it, but Mr. Brownleigh's unpleasant death prevented the auction. I did not like Mr. Brownleigh, but I did not wish his death. But he is dead, and someone stole the manuscript. That does not mean that I do not still wish to own Jayne's second work. I will buy the manuscript from whoever has it. I will ask no questions, and I will remain silent about that person's name. I am not a policeman and I am not a judge. I cannot say, and none of you can say, that justice has not already been done. Perhaps it was Mr. Brownleigh's death that was necessary to restore order to the universe. I will be in my room waiting for a call to arrange transfer of the manuscript and of your fee."

I was struck speechless.

Megan, however, seldom has that problem. "Dr. Yahara, I sympathize with your point of view. Everyone wants the manuscript and no one much liked Brownleigh, and while I value life, I'll agree that perhaps Brownleigh aided the cause of his own death by being such a slimeball while living. The problem is that once a person murders for gain, he or she finds it much easier to murder a second time. In other words, you may now be a target, because I'm sure that any sale will be for cash, and what's to keep the murderer from grabbing the cash and doing his revised version of Cheating the Hangman on you?"

There was silence in the room again while everyone added imagery to Megan's scenario: a dark parking lot somewhere, a masked figure dressed in black, the luminescence of a sunflower-yellow string, a struggle, and Dr. Yahara lying dead on the asphalt.

I didn't much care for my image, and judging by the looks on the faces of others in the room, their images weren't any more cheerful. The fact is that Dr. Yahara was proposing to pay a reward to a murderer, and that left a bad taste in everyone's mouth.

"Dr. Yahara, I would like to visit with you a moment." It was everybody's favorite cop, Lieutenant Jerry Carr, eavesdropping again. We were going to have to start taking turns standing guard at the door to warn of the approach of the law.

Dr. Yahara looked apprehensive. "Mr. Jackson, sir, if you are available to advise me?"

Herb stood up, rearranged his *Host* badge over the leather vest he wore over his convention T-shirt, and with real regret shook his head. "I'm sorry, Dr. Yahara, but I have been retained by Ms. Hobbs, and I cannot ethically represent more than one client on the same case."

"Don't worry, Dr. Yahara, Ryan and I will accompany you to the Yucca Room," Megan offered, her eyes narrowed into amber-colored slits. "Or were you planning to take Dr. Yahara downtown to Special Crimes, Jerry?"

If I had been Jerry, I would have backed off at that point. Anytime an amber-colored sliver is all you can see of Megan Clark's eyes, she's on a rampage, and she comes from a long line of rampaging women. I remember her mother backing down Department of Energy bureaucrats, standing on her front porch, tapping her foot, and reading a list of demands for the benefit of the bureaucrats and the media, but mostly the media. She was masterful at handling the media. Some politician lost a fine press secretary, provided the politician made her short list—which I think had maybe five names on it, two being Washington and Lincoln. I also heard my mother mention that Megan's great-grandmother was a leader in the women's suffrage movement during WWI and after, until the constitutional amendment giving women the vote passed. But you get my point. Megan is stubborn, tenacious, determined, and whatever other adjective you might want to use, and she comes by it naturally.

Jerry looked at the ceiling, but I could have told him there were no answers there. "I guess I can visit with Dr. Yahara in the Yucca Room, but I don't need your or Dr. Stevens's help. You're not attorneys."

Megan opened her eyes as wide as they would go. "Oh, does he need an attorney, Jerry? Is he a suspect in the Brownleigh murder case. If he's a suspect, then you must read him his rights, and I'll tell him not to say one word—*nada, rien*—until I call my mother to get another of her lawyer cronies. I have one in mind. He's nearly as obnoxious as the one who's representing me."

I could almost sympathize with Jerry. I could see him turning over his options in his mind and discarding them one by one, until finally, he capitulated. "Come on, Megan, Dr. Stevens, you can make sure I don't use rubber hoses."

Dr. Yahara looked alarmed. "What's this? I heard

about rubber hoses in one of your George Raft movies."

Megan took his arm. "Never mind, Dr. Yahara, it was a joke and it didn't make it through the translation."

He still looked somewhat alarmed as we followed Jerry Carr into the Yucca Room. The recording equipment was still in place on top of the banquet table, and one of Jerry's henchman sat at one end. Actually, she was a henchwoman, but I'm speaking generically.

Jerry motioned us to sit, which we did, one on either side of Dr. Yahara so he would feel protected against the law. Jerry sat opposite us and rubbed his temples with his fingertips. I thought he must have had a headache.

"Megan! One of these days I am going to throw you in jail for interference and I don't care what my mother says. She doesn't know you like I do." He took a tin of aspirin out of his pocket and swallowed a couple dry. "You have managed to mess up what I thought was a really good plan, but then I guess I should have known better than to plan anything when you're within a hundred miles."

Megan looked bewildered. It was an expression I had so seldom seen on her face that I barely recognized it. "What plan? What are you talking about, Jerry?"

Dr. Yahara looked apologetic. "I am so sorry, Dr. Megan Clark, but I volunteered to work undercover for Lieutenant Carr. I was supposed to make my offer to buy the manuscript, then the lieutenant would step in and arrest the murderer when he showed up for an exchange. I am sorry, Lieutenant Jerry Carr, that I made my offer when you were in the room. You had no choice but to arrest me, or in your expression, the cat was out of the bag. But your plan may work yet. I can make my offer again to show the murderers that I am not afraid of you."

"And I didn't have a choice but to go in the Hospitality Room once I saw Megan entering. If I had not arrested you, then Dr. Clark here would have been hiding out trying to catch the murderer herself. If she hadn't chewed you up and spit you out for encouraging theft and murder by making such an offer in the first place. I had to tell you to keep you from interfering, Megan," said Jerry.

Megan was silent. If I didn't know better, I would think she was speechless, but I told you earlier that speechless was practically an impossibility in her case. She was just mentally arranging her thoughts before she jumped on the lieutenant.

"As Dr. Yahara says, the plan may work yet—not as well as it would have worked had you had the decency to tell me first," said Megan.

"It has nothing to do with decency," said Jerry Carr in the tone of a yelp. He nearly yelped literally. "I didn't want another civilian involved in this investigation."

"You think I'm not involved already? What do you call sitting with a corpse whose eyes bulged? If you had trusted me in the first place, Jerry, we wouldn't be in this trouble." Megan was on a tear, and I was enjoying it.

"All right, all right, so now you know, and I'm sorry I didn't trust you. Will you get off my back and quit threatening me with those loudmouthed attorneys. I'd rather walk down a street covered in shattered plate glass in my bare feet than listen to those two blowhards. But back to you, Dr. Yahara. I would like for you to wear a wire so any conversation you have with the thief is on tape and we can do a voice-print on him."

"So, I will be wired," said Dr. Yahara with a grin. "Such an adventure in search of justice."

"I don't know about that," said Megan. "I wore a wire once when Ryan and I caught a murderer. It was really uncomfortable."

"We bought the wire at RadioShack, and you're built differently from Dr. Yahara," I said, glad to finally contribute to the conversation. From the way Megan glared at me, I should have kept my mouth shut. This murder was making her touchier than the last one we were involved in.

Megan and I left Dr. Yahara in Jerry Carr's and Sony's capable hands and walked back to the Apache Door Hospitality Room. No sooner had we left the Yucca Room than Megan jumped me. "What have you found out from Denise? Quick, tell me."

"That she has more hands than an octopus."

"What?"

"That woman hasn't said a word to me about

Thursday night. She's all hands, Megan. I'm lucky not to have been raped."

"Actually, while a man can be sexually molested, I've never believed that he could actually be raped because it would require some physical response on his part."

"I resent that!"

"I'm sorry, Ryan, that was a sexist remark and I apologize."

"You ought to be. And that Denise! I thought a radical feminist wouldn't like men, and I was worried about how I would approach her to gain her confidence."

"Apparently, you succeeded." Megan tried to smother what I clearly heard as laughter.

"It's not funny, Megan! I swear that when I get home tonight I'm going to stand in the shower until the hot water runs out, just to get rid of the smell of her perfume. And it's all been useless. She never said a word to me."

"Keep trying, Ryan, please. There is a reason for that thirty-minute difference between her story and mine."

"Maybe she just forgot. Did you ever think of that? I mean, why does everything have to be so complicated?"

"Because this is real life, Ryan. Things are simple only in books."

We walked into the Apache Door Hospitality Room, and into a flood of questions. Megan reassured everyone that she and I persuaded Lieutenant

Carr that he had no evidence against Dr. Yahara, but that if the good doctor did buy the manuscript, he would be guilty of suppressing evidence, and would be sent to prison to share a cell with Guido, the three-hundred-pound biker. Everyone acted as if they believed her, which owed more to her red hair and freckles than to her veracity. I just shook my head as though the experience had been so terrible that I couldn't talk about it.

That didn't discourage LeClerc, who went about her business of pawing me. I did notice Megan glaring at her, which for just a moment made me think she was jealous, but soon realized it was just her reaction to Denise's comments, half of which I missed in the hubbub of fighting off her roaming fingers.

"—a woman, she would have been held in jail without bail, but because Yahara is a man, he is let go with only a stern warning." It didn't take much intelligence to figure out that Denise was hacked that Yahara wasn't already in the cell with Guido, the three-hundred-pound biker.

But we weren't finished with quixotic efforts to recover the missing manuscript. The Reverend Wilson took the pulpit, or rather the floor in front of the cocktail table. "I want to urge the thief to confess his sins and render up the manuscript."

I noticed that nobody seemed too concerned about Brownleigh's murder, because the reverend didn't say a word about the murderer coming forward. I was beginning to hope that the manuscript would never be found because the desire to own it was turning some decent people into less than nice. One could only speculate what would happen if the manuscript were actually found. I remembered the Battle of the Sagebrush Room, and shuddered.

"As a minister, I want to encourage you to give up the manuscript. It will only bring you unhappiness because it was obtained in a sinful manner. I am so anxious for you to turn in the manuscript, not only for the good of your eternal soul, but so it might be given to the Center of Cultural Studies on Nauru Island. In this way, the inhabitants might recapture some of their lost culture. It is a worthy cause and would expiate some of your sin. I will be in my room for the next hour and will welcome you and pray with you."

"Nice appeal, but I don't think the killer will be accepting, do you?" whispered Denise, breathing down my collar.

I decided I should do what I should have done this morning. "How did you manage to steal that manuscript page from Brownleigh," I whispered back. "You know, the one you slipped into Candi Hobbs's purse."

"How did you know it was me?" she asked, drawing back a little—not enough, but any distance was better than none.

"Candi screamed like a banshee when she found that page. If she had known it was in there, she would have quietly sneaked into the ladies' room and tucked it somewhere under her clothing. Therefore, she didn't know. You were sitting next to her, and you had reason to be angry at her, and saw that page as a way to get her into more trouble than she could handle. So you slipped it in her purse. What I want to know is how you got the page in the first place."

"It was simple. I mocked up a page after I heard from the others what the manuscript looked like, and switched the pages while I was examining them. If someone hadn't killed Brownleigh, I would have had an authentic page of the lost Caroline Furness Jayne manuscript. As it was, I had to get rid of it, and I had a good reason to be angry with Candi Hobbs. If I had had two pages, I would have given the other one to Randal Anderson—but I didn't." She smiled at me and ruffled my hair. I don't mind women running their hands through my hair—at least, I still have a full head of it—but I like to choose the woman in whose hands I place my head and any other body part she might be interested in.

I would not choose Denise LeClerc.

"And I suppose you told the lieutenant that you saw Megan Clark at one o'clock, when you actually saw her at twelve-thirty just to get her into trouble."

She leaned back (she was sprawled nearly in my lap) and smiled. "Perhaps that was my reason. After all, she never made Candi Hobbs apologize."

"So who did you see at one o'clock?" I asked, scooting toward the edge of the couch so I could get up and escape her clutches.

She got a death lock around my neck and proceeded to nibble my ear. "Dear, sweet Dr. Stevens, what makes you think I saw anyone at one o'clock?"

I clasped her wrists and unwound her arms from my neck, then got up. "You're playing games with a murderer, Denise, and that's very, very dangerous."

"I don't think so, Ryan. Not in this case."

13

If there was anything worse than getting what one didn't deserve, it was getting in full what one did deserve.

—CORPORAL JACK BUTLER, in Anthony Price's
The '44 Vintage, 1978

Megan saw Ryan and Denise in deep conversation, and hoped that he was finally tending to business. She could tell that Denise made it difficult with her constant groping. Poor Ryan. She would have thought that a man who came of age during the seventies and the sexual revolution would not get so flustered by female aggression. On the other hand, Ryan was pretty old-fashioned, and Denise had long since passed simple aggression and was now into molestation. He glanced toward Megan with an expression in his eyes that was clearly an appeal for help. Poor Ryan. On top of his allergies to horses, which so embarrassed his ranching family, he was also a gentleman. Any man of Megan's generation would have long since escaped Denise's grasping hands by throwing up, if no other way.

Megan started across the room to Ryan's rescue when she heard David Owen Lister (his name did sound so much like a mouthwash) tear into the reverend with a vengeance.

"If you want to pray for the thief, or pray with him for that matter, that's fine, Reverend, but don't think you'll get that manuscript for a prayer. Not only that, I object to your whole agenda. There is more to that manuscript than instructions for Nauru string figures. That manuscript needs to be published and made available to the world, not stuck away in some dusty case in a two-bit museum on an island on the ass end of nowhere."

"Young man, I object to your tone of voice. You are being irreverent toward the power of prayer," said Reverend Wilson.

"I'm not being irreverent. I'm being relevant, and what's relevant here is that you are a trustee of the Center of Cultural Studies on Nauru Island. I know because you passed out brochures about the center, and guess who's listed in the small print on the back? Reverend Robert Wilson, Anglican priest."

There was an explosion of voices, loudest among them that of Denise. "You're a faker, old man."

Rosemary and Lorene looked disappointed, as if their illusions about the reverend had been tarnished.

But missionaries, whether they be Catholic or Protestant, are tougher than most people think, as Megan knew from the number of preachers who fought for her mother's various causes, and the Reverend Wilson took up his own defense. "That I happen to be a trustee does not negate the worthiness of the center.

To restore a part of the Nauru Islanders' lost culture is a wonderful goal."

"Oh, I agree," said Lister. "But I think you ought to be up front with us about being a trustee. I certainly wouldn't object to donating the manuscript to the center, once it's in print for the rest of the world to enjoy."

"That's if the thief comes forward, young man. Unless *you* are the thief."

"Hey, don't talk like that with the cops here. I didn't murder anyone and I didn't steal the manuscript."

Denise LeClerc showed herself to be a true radical feminist as she deserted Ryan (and his body) for an argument. "You," she said in her loud, high-pitched voice, pointing at David, "you only want the manuscript for the money you'll make. And you"—she whipped her finger around to point at Reverend Wilson—"you represent a male-dominated religion that will subvert a woman's work for the amusement of the Nauru men."

"I—I—I have never been so insulted and neither has my God," stuttered the reverend.

"God is not insulted," replied Denise. "I asked Her."

"Blasphemy, woman, you speak blasphemy!"

"I have never understood why anyone found it necessary to change God into a woman," said Rosemary.

David Owen Lister was not cowed by Denise either. "Hey, I'm the only bidder who guarantees to publish the manuscript, and you better believe I'll keep my word because it is the only way to recoup my money."

"Young woman, you know God is not a man, if you're angry with men, which you seem to be. God is God, not a man," said Lorene.

"Dr. LeClerc, I don't see the necessity of bringing religion into this discussion," said Dr. Moser. "This is about an anthropological artifact."

Denise whirled to face Dr. Moser where he sat on the couch. She flung up her hand in what Megan thought was a nasty little gesture. "Dr. Moser would make a shrine out of Jayne's manuscript and expect everyone to genuflect each time he or she was in the presence of the work. Women have had enough of the pedestal, Dr. Moser. Caroline Furness Jayne can do without your Victorian idolatry. Give me the manuscript so that she may finally receive the credit she deserves without male condescension."

Dr. Moser did not move, but Megan saw the blood rush to his face, then recede, leaving him looking both gray and his age. "Young woman, do you know what you are asking?"

Denise LeClerc straightened to her full height. "Yes, Dr. Moser, I do."

"Then you are unspeakable."

"You crazy old man, don't call me names!"

Megan climbed on the cocktail table for the second time in two days. "SHUT UP!" she shouted. Once quiet descended, she cleared her throat. "The next paper to be delivered will be 'The Cat's Cradle from Asia to England: Patterns of Human Migration As

Revealed by This Common String Figure.' It will be delivered by John Harper in the Sagebrush Room. I'm sure we're all looking forward to John's presentation."

"I suppose you'll quote from *String Figures and How to Make Them*," said Denise, her face flushed from her previous arguments.

"Yes, I will," said John Harper. "Her book is the bible of string figures."

"You're attempting to turn Caroline Furness Jayne into dry statistics with no credit for her womanness."

"I don't believe womanness is a word," said John. "Did you just make it up?"

Megan reached for the pitcher of ice water.

"That's enough!" said Ryan in a thunderous voice Megan remembered his using when she and his four children got in a fight with a family down the street. Funny how she had forgotten.

"That's enough picking at one another. We are civilized and for the most part highly educated people. I believe we can walk across to the Sagebrush Room and listen to Mr. Harper's paper without any further conversation, and certainly without any further argumentative language."

Ryan opened the sliding-glass doors at the front of the room and stood aside. "Out!" he called, pointing across the open space toward the Sagebrush Room.

Megan passed him. "Hey, that was quite a performance for a mild-mannered history professor. Let's go listen to John's paper, and watch the string-figure demonstrations, and you can tell me what you learned from Denise."

"Not much. She switched a fake page for a real one during her appointment, then slipped it into Candi's purse when the cops started searching everyone's belongings. She didn't tell me a thing about who she saw at one o'clock, but whoever it was, she's not afraid of him. Now you know all I know, and I'm heading for the only place where Denise can't follow me. The men's room!"

"I wouldn't count on it," said Megan.

Sitting in the back where she could slip out if chairwoman duties called, Megan scanned the audience in the Sagebrush Room, but didn't see Ryan. He must still be hiding in the men's room, she decided, but how long could he do that before the management thought there might be something a bit off with him and call the cops? Most men lurking in a public bathroom for several hours were candidates for arrest for a variety of sexual offenses. If he didn't come out soon, she would send in Dr. Moser to talk him out.

Megan glanced down at her revised program. The next demonstrator was David Owen Lister, who would make A Parrot Cage from Yorubu, West Africa, a complex figure found in Kathleen Haddon's book, *Cat's Cradles from Many Lands*. After David's presentation, Dr. Moser would demonstrate the Apache Door along with several of its variations. Megan definitely wanted to watch Dr. Moser and take notes. Perhaps she could do a paper on the Apache

Door if she could think of a way to relate all the variations to a single theme. Maybe the *Smithsonian* would buy it.

Following Dr. Moser was John Harper making the figure, Storm Clouds, from Caroline Furness Jayne's first book. Megan was interested in that figure also, because it had several variations. Last on the program was everyone's favorite person: Denise LeClerc. Megan wondered why anyone would be as deliberately unpleasant as Denise. Did such unpleasantness bring her satisfaction in some way? Did she need to be unpleasant to hide an underlying personality defect? Maybe she had some physical disorder that warped her personality, like the Egyptian pharaoh, Akhenaten, whose odd appearance ensured that he did not participate in public ceremonies. Since almost all ceremonies in ancient Egypt were religious, Akhenaten grew up to despise the priests and Egypt's multiple gods, thus explaining why he overthrew both, built a new capital, and declared Aten the only god. If he had been born without his particular affliction, the history of Egypt might have been very different.

Somehow Megan didn't think Denise LeClerc could offer affliction as an excuse for her bad manners, but there was no way to tell without an autopsy—which couldn't be performed on a living person, and Denise looked healthy enough to last several more decades.

Jerry Carr slipped into the chair next to Megan. "So how are the demonstrations going?"

"Fine, if your presence doesn't scare the presenters. What are you doing in here anyway?"

"It's as good as any other place when your investigation has stalled," he said, stretching out his legs in the aisle.

Megan stared up at him, surprised that he would admit it. "Everyone has motive, means, and opportunity, so that's the same as saying anybody could do it, and nobody is more likely than the next person. So where do you go from here?"

He glanced down at her. "Back to Special Crimes, I guess. Put my feet up on my desk, go over my notes, and realize that the best suspect I have is you, and I don't think you would kill anyone. Besides the pathologist called with the preliminary autopsy results, and his ballpark figure on how long Brownleigh was kicked before he died was thirty minutes to an hour. That was as close as he could get. He also warned me to be careful around you."

"What about Dr. Yahara's wire? Any luck there?" asked Megan, ignoring Jerry's attempt at humor.

"Yeah, another guest asked if he was looking over the motel because a Japanese business group wanted to buy it, because if they did, he wanted to report that the toilet in Room 128 leaked, and they should make the current ownership pay for having it fixed. Other than that, nothing. Oh, the other folks at the convention talked to him, but it's all in string-figure language, so it's Greek to me, but nobody offered to buy the manuscript. The closest anyone got to mentioning it is Denise LeClerc, who called Dr. Yahara an example of a male-dominated society, who would share the manuscript only with other men."

"That sounds like Denise," said Megan. "She's managed to insult everyone at the convention, some of them twice."

"Excuse me, Dr. Clark, but could I possibly prevail upon you to order us an urn of coffee. It's the middle of the afternoon, and everyone is yawning. I always hate it when my audience sleeps through my demonstrations. I never know if the audience is particularly tired, or if I'm particularly boring." Dr. Moser leaned on his cane as he spoke. Megan noticed that his color was still not good, being more of a grayish tone than a healthy pink.

She laid aside her notebook and got up. "I'll get your urn of coffee, Dr. Moser. Why don't you sit here and rest while I'm gone."

Dr. Moser leaned even more heavily on his cane, until Megan worried that the old man might topple over. "I don't want to take your seat, my dear. You won't be gone that long."

"I might," said Megan. "I have to persuade Dr. Stevens to come out of the men's room."

"I saw him in there an hour ago," said Dr. Moser. "He was sitting on the floor by the door, asking everyone who came in if Denise LeClerc was anywhere in sight. I told him she was in the Sagebrush Room and settled for a while, but he said he'd wait a little longer. He made me promise not to mention his presence, although every man who steps through the door sees him. He's afraid word of his whereabouts will get back to Denise—although no one is talking to her any more than necessary—and that she'll materialize next to the urinals."

"The doc is hiding out from the dragon LeClerc?" asked Jerry.

"Yes, what about it?" asked Megan, ready to defend Ryan's honor if necessary.

"I'd stay in the men's room if I was him," said Jerry. "I arrested a serial killer once who had better manners than she has, and outside of his quirk of killing every man he saw who had a tattoo, he might have been a better person." He paused a moment, a thoughtful look on his face. "We never did figure out what it was about a tattoo that set him off."

"Jerry, I don't think Denise is a serial killer, and I don't think it's healthy either physically or mentally to hide out in a men's room. I'm getting Ryan out of there if I have to go in after him."

As she walked out she overheard Jerry tell Dr. Moser that "the poor guy doesn't have a chance against Megan Clark, and nobody else has a chance against him." Megan wondered why people persisted in seeing some kind of romantic attachment between Ryan and her, when their relationship was the purest kind of friendship.

Megan ordered the coffee, then walked down the hall to the men's room. She knocked on the door, not that she thought Ryan would answer, but to give any other man who might be in there a chance to zip up. There was silence, so she pushed open the door and walked in. "Ryan, come out, come out wherever you are," she sang.

There was a thud as two feet appeared under a stall door, and Ryan peeked out. "What are you doing in the men's room? Get out of here! What if a man comes in?"

"Well, I wouldn't expect a woman to come in unless it was Denise LeClerc, whom I am going to inform that you are in here, if you don't come out right now! This is silly, Ryan. You're a grown man, a full professor, you can handle an overage, overweight flirt."

Ryan came out of the stall, a panicked expression on his face. "She's not a flirt! A flirt is one of my students who winks at me. This woman is a full column of tanks after one man in a little red wagon. I can't help it, Megan. I don't know what to do. If Denise were a man, I would deck her, and that would be the end of it. But I can't hit a woman, even a woman like Denise. I'm bigger than she is, not by much, but it's the principle of the thing. A decent man doesn't hit a woman, period, end of sentence, all she wrote."

Denise's obnoxious behavior was giving Megan a whole different perspective on sexual harassment, and she decided to write her congressman about a review of the laws defining it. Better yet, she would tell her mother.

But for the moment she just held out her hand. "Come on, Ryan. You're with me, and everyone knows it but Denise, and she will if she puts a finger on you again."

Ryan stiffened and squared his shoulders. "I can't hide behind a woman's skirts."

"I'm not wearing skirts; I'm wearing carpenter's pants. And under today's laws, you don't have a choice. Not many people are willing to believe a man can be sexually harassed. What can I say? Our culture is crazy right now. But it will correct itself, or at least, that's been the historic pattern."

Ryan took her hand, pulled her into his arms, and rubbed his cheek against the top of her head. "That's why I'm a history professor. I like our past culture better than the present. And I'm glad I've got you, Megan."

Megan stood still in his arms, not sure what he might do next, and what was worse, not sure what she would do about whatever he did. If he kissed her, would she kiss him back? She was very, very afraid that she would. Then what would happen to their platonic relationship? What did she want to happen to it? She wasn't sure. Sometimes men were so much trouble.

"Hey! You two perverts get out of the rest rooms to do your necking! Jeez, buddy, can't you afford a room?" A tall man, his paunch bisected by a belt with a cheap Western buckle big enough to hold a chicken-fried steak and fries, stood glaring at them.

Megan felt her face go beyond red and into the purple shades. "Sorry, we didn't mean to offend you," Ryan told the man as he tightened his arms around her and shuffled toward the door.

Outside, Megan pulled loose from his arms, leaned

against the wall, and laughed until she felt tears rolling down her still-red cheeks. "I've never been called a pervert before, Ryan."

"I haven't either, but I've had a lot of new experiences since I met you—after you were grown up and came back to Amarillo," he added as if she wouldn't know what he meant. She wasn't sure she did anyway.

"I want to watch Dr. Moser make the Apache Door and it's variations," Megan said, taking Ryan's hand again. "Walk me to the Sagebrush Room."

"I'll do better than that. I'll go in with you and watch him, too. I'm going to stick to you like a burr on a pair of britches. I figure it's the only way I won't be pounced on by Denise."

Megan was still giggling when she and Ryan slipped in the Sagebrush Room and sat down next to Jerry Carr. "Did we miss much?"

"I don't know," said Jerry, pointing toward the front of the room, where John Harper, Dr. Moser, and Denise LeClerc shared the podium. "Those three have been alternating performances, if that's what you call making string figures. You know, it's kind of interesting when you watch and listen for a while. I never knew there was much to it once you made a Cat's Cradle."

"There's enough to it that somebody murdered Clyde Brownleigh just to steal an old manuscript about how to make some obscure string figures from an island culture that probably never had a population over twenty-five hundred in the history of its existence. Most people don't even know where Nauru Island is."

Megan realized she sounded bitter, but bitter was how she felt. No one, at least among the string-figure enthusiasts, seemed to remember that somebody deliberately and with malice aforethought, as the term went, strangled Brownleigh to death. He wasn't lovable, he wasn't even likable, but he must have had a mother who loved him at least a little bit. He was slimy and crude, lewd and disgusting, but Megan felt guilty for kicking him. But how was she to know he would have a sunflower-yellow cord pulled tight around his neck thirty minutes—or so—later? She couldn't. No one could except the man or woman who did the pulling. Which brought up an interesting point.

"Jerry, Denise told Ryan that she wasn't afraid of whomever she saw at one o'clock," Megan began.

"Look at how much bigger she is than you, Megan. She must outweigh you by a hundred pounds, and she's at least eight inches taller. If she believes you're the murderer, I can see why she's not afraid," said Jerry.

"Will you please stop interrupting me?" Megan demanded quietly. "What I was going to say before you assumed you knew, was that Denise admitted she saw me at twelve-thirty, but she wouldn't tell Ryan whom she saw at one. Now, isn't it just possible that the reason she's not afraid of whomever she saw at one is that she's the person who went into Brownleigh's room. She admitted slipping the manuscript page into

Candi's purse, but told Ryan she had switched a fake page for a real one while examining the manuscript. Rosemary and Lorene told me that Brownleigh laid two pages on the desk and watched each person examine them. I'm not saying that Denise couldn't have switched the pages, but if she didn't, then she has the manuscript, which means she killed Brownleigh at one o'clock or soon thereafter. Doesn't that make sense?"

Jerry gazed at Denise sitting on the left side of Dr. Moser, watching the old professor make the Apache Door while her supercilious expression said as clearly as words that whatever he could do, she could do better.

Finally, Jerry turned to look at Megan and whispered, "It makes enough sense that I'll want to talk to Dr. Dragon Lady again."

"I'll slip up to the podium and give her a note, saying you'll be waiting for her at the door as soon as her demonstration is over," said Megan.

Ryan saw her rise and grabbed her hand. "You're not leaving me, are you?"

She patted his hand as she freed her own. "I've just made an appointment for Denise with Jerry Carr so she can explain to him how she got that manuscript page. I'm going up to the podium to give her a note."

Ryan sighed. "She'll know I ratted her out."

"Ratted her out? Ryan, I wish you would stop watching those films noirs on TV. Your vocabulary is peppered with colorful but decidedly out-of-date underworld slang."

Megan shook her head and walked up to the podium to give Denise notice of her upcoming appointment.

"What do you mean by this?" Denise demanded in a loud whisper, shaking the note in Megan's face.

Megan could hear the audience stir and mutter behind her. Quickly she turned around. "We'll have a fifteen-minute break, then our presenters will continue their demonstrations." Just as quickly she turned back to Denise. "If you don't want the whole convention to know your business, keep your voice down. Jerry Carr wants to talk to you again about what you saw while allegedly loitering in the hall Thursday night when Brownleigh was murdered."

Dr. Moser and John Harper were looking at the ceiling or examining their loops of string, anything to give the impression that they were ignoring the discussion. They weren't, of course; no one in the audience was. David Owen Lister and Dr. Yahara were staring at the podium, leaning forward as people will when eavesdropping. Reverend Robert Wilson nudged Rosemary and Lorene as if to say, "See, I knew she was up to no good."

The other members of the Murder by the Yard Reading Circle didn't move either. In fact, Megan saw Candi Hobbs taking notes as fast as if she were a recording secretary for a ladies' club.

"What do you mean, allegedly?" demanded Denise, her voice pitched even higher until it squeaked like a badly played violin.

"That's the word used when a witness's story hasn't been corroborated by evidence," whispered Megan, hoping that Denise would get the point and lower her own voice.

Denise, however, didn't take the hint. "It was Dr. Stevens who betrayed me, wasn't it?"

"Don't be melodramatic, Denise. Ryan only asked you a few questions, which you answered of your own free will. You knew all along he was my friend and Candi's friend. He was trying to find out the truth. Clyde Brownleigh was murdered! Does that not mean anything to you, or to anyone at this convention?"

"Dr. Clark," said Dr. Moser. "I believe we might as well go on with our presentations. I don't believe the audience has moved from their chairs, and I don't think they intend to, either. Dr. Yahara, could I impose upon you to bring us a carafe of coffee from the urn. Our cups are empty, and I believe the three of us could use a caffeine lift."

"That's what I like to see, a man serving a woman for once," said Denise.

"Please, Dr. LeClerc, must you be rude?" asked Dr. Moser.

Megan used the interval to walk back to her seat. Let Dr. Moser chastise Denise. He would probably be better at it anyway. After all, he had decades of experience with unruly students, and Denise was definitely unruly along with several other behavioral faults.

Denise opened her carrying case and began taking out loops of string, holding several in her mouth as she sorted through the colors. "I'll thank him when he pours my coffee. That's the extent of my good manners today," she mumbled around the string.

"Dr. Moser, your coffee. I will pour it myself so I will not give offense to Dr. LeClerc by refusing to serve her," said Dr. Yahara. "To the Japanese, manners are very important."

Dr. Moser pushed the three coffee cups toward Dr. Yahara, who carefully filled each one, and bowed to each person as he handed them their coffee. Megan thought it was a most exquisite put-down of Denise LeClerc, and vowed to hug Dr. Yahara at the first opportunity. Or perhaps bow to him, as he was such a reserved gentleman.

Denise spit out her loops of string, took a slurp of her coffee, then picked up a luminescent white cord. "I believe I'm next. I will be constructing the Moon Goes Dark, a continuation of the figure called the Moon, which is found in several different cultures." She paused for another sip of coffee, then grimaced and bent over suddenly. She straightened and stared out at the audience. "I will be constructing the Moon Goes Dark, a continuation of the figure called the Moon, which is found in several different cultures."

"Dr. LeClerc, you've already told us that," said Dr. Moser in a soft voice.

Denise giggled, then laughed, ending by panting.

"I'm just a little behind myself right now. Ho, ho, ho, here's how you make the Moon. Watch me now."

Megan heard murmurs from the audience as Denise's eyelids began to twitch. "What's wrong with her? Is she drunk?" she heard Randal Anderson ask.

After several attempts, Denise managed to make Opening A. "I did it, I did it, I did it," she chanted, letting her hands fall to the tabletop as if she could no longer hold them up.

John Harper leaned around Dr. Moser's back. "Denise, are you sick?"

"No! No, no, no, no," she sang between deep breaths as she managed to lift her hands to her mouth and seize 5f with her teeth. She sat there, sucking the string with a look of wide-eyed idiocy on her face, then her face and hands began twitching, and then she suddenly fell sideways out of her chair.

14

CUP AND SAUCER

A string figure believed to have originated in New Caledonia, but is now found worldwide, thanks to international trade.

1. Opening A.

2. R1 and L1 (Right Thumb and Left Thumb) picks up far string on L2 and R2 (Right and Left far Index Finger strings) and extends.

3. Navaho (Seize with your teeth) the *lower* R1 and L1 loop over the *upper* R1 and L1 loop and release. Extend.

4. Release the R5 and L5 loops and extend.

I figured Denise had suffered a stroke. Nobody can be filled with so much bile without it doing her in eventually. Jerry Carr was out of his seat, desperately pulling a cell phone from his pocket and dialing 911 at the same time as he was pushing through the crowd that had also rushed from their seats to the podium. I followed Jerry because I figured—God Almighty, I don't know what I figured. I guess I was a sheep following the flock.

I saw Megan disappearing into the crowd and heard a few exclamations of pain, so I figured she was making her way through the throng in her usual efficient fashion. Megan wears hiking boots most of the time when she's not working at the library, and if you've never had your toes stomped on by somebody wearing hiking boots, I recommend that you avoid it if at all possible. Of course, Megan is not above kicking shins either, if she feels her goal is important enough. Apparently in this case she did, because I saw one or two attendees duck down to check out the damage to their lower extremities.

She made it to the podium before Jerry or I was halfway there, and grabbed the microphone off the lectern. "EVERYBODY SIT DOWN AND LET LIEUTENANT CARR AND DR. STEVENS THROUGH. DR. LECLERC IS HAVING CONVULSIONS, AND WE DON'T NEED ANYBODY GAWKING AND GETTING IN THE WAY."

Megan has a certain authority about her even though she is short, particularly when she's shouting into a microphone. Most of the audience dropped into the nearest chair and clapped their hands over their ears. Jerry Carr and I winced and lumbered onto the podium. Dr. Moser and John Harper, assisted by Megan, were trying to hold down Denise LeClerc, who was convulsing into shapes as complex as any string figure. Jerry and I dropped to our knees and each grabbed an arm and shoulder. John Harper was lying across her legs in an attempt to still them, but Denise's violent motions bounced him up and down. Dr.

Moser was attempting to hold down her head to prevent her from repeatedly slamming it against the wooden podium. Megan gestured him away.

"I'll take over, Dr. Moser," she said, and grabbed the end of the tablecloth on the banquet table that served as lectern. She wadded it up into a ropelike shape and stuffed it between Denise's teeth.

"Does anyone know if she has epilepsy?" I asked. "Is this a grand mal seizure?"

Megan was staring at the inside of Denise's mouth. "No, it's poison."

Suddenly Denise gasped several times, her eyes took on a fixed expression, and she died. I didn't have to check her pulse to know she died. You can see it in the eyes. They become lifeless. I wonder sometimes, when it's late at night and I'm not sleeping well, and thoughts of my deceased wife bring memories of her death, I wonder if life leaves us, not when the heart stops or the brain dies, but when our eyes die. Is that the moment that our soul leaves our body?

Whether the body dies first or the soul departs first, Denise LeClerc was dead by both criteria.

"How do you know she was poisoned?" asked Jerry Carr as he released Denise and signaled for me and John Harper to do the same.

Megan removed the tablecloth from between Denise's teeth, and using a corner of the pristine white fabric, opened Denise's mouth as wide as possible and tilted her head back. "Look at the burn marks on the tissues. I can't see any further down her throat without tongue depressors and a light, but I'm betting that they will also show corrosive burning. Don't touch that string!" she suddenly shouted at John Harper, who was trying to pick up the loops of string Denise had dropped when she collapsed.

John dropped the string like it was a hot coal and started wiping his hands on his shirt. "What is it? What killed her?"

Megan leaned over and sniffed Denise's mouth, then examined her hands, checking each finger and the palm. Then she checked her arms and ran a finger around the collar of Denise's convention T-shirt. Finally, she looked up. "Without toxicology tests, I can't be sure, but I smell tobacco and Denise didn't smoke—or didn't that I ever saw—and her fingers and nails lack any of the yellow nicotine stains that a smoker almost inevitably has. I think she died of nicotine poisoning, and it was murder. No one knowingly takes nicotine poison, but it's a wonderful murder weapon. I'm surprised more people don't use it for that purpose. It is tasteless, easily absorbed by the skin—that's why I didn't want you touching her string, John. We don't know how she ingested the nicotine, but it has to be either from the string or the coffee. Nicotine poisoning works very quickly and very effectively. It's an alkaloid, naturally occurring in plants and fungi, and is in the same group of poisons as morphine, strychnine, and aconitine."

We were all silent for a moment, digesting that information, pardon the pun.

"But we all drank the coffee," said Dr. Moser.

"And I don't feel any worse than I usually do. At ninety-six you can't ever say you feel good—just alive."

"Jerry, bag those coffee cups for the lab," said Megan. "And the loops of strings. If you have a chemist on call, he can find the nicotine pretty quickly, faster than the pathologist can. The poison has already been absorbed into the body, and it'll take time to filter it back out. But at least the pathologist and the chemist know what they're looking for. That smell of tobacco is unmistakable, particularly since she wasn't a smoker. If she had been, well, it might have been several days before we knew what killed her."

Megan rose to her knees, patted Denise on the shoulder, and got up. "I couldn't stand that woman, but I didn't want to see her dead."

I rose, too, very steady under the circumstances. I mean, I was shaken, but there was no blood, so I didn't faint. I believe I mentioned earlier my aversion to blood—mine or anyone else's.

Jerry's Special Crimes techs came in along with the justice of the peace for this precinct. I don't believe I've ever mentioned that in Texas it is the precinct justice of the peace who pronounces a person dead, orders an autopsy, and has charge of the body and the evidence until such a time as he turns over authority to Special Crimes. Some JPs use their authority to the hilt, and others sweep the body with a glance, order an autopsy, and they're gone. This particular JP fell somewhere between the two extremes, mainly because he was on one of Megan's mother's boards for one cause or another, and wanted to impress Megan. He was harmless enough, I guess, although Jerry Carr gritted his perfect white teeth and jutted out his Dick Tracy jaw in frustration while the old man poked and prodded Denise's corpse, nodded as Megan gave him the exact time and probable cause of death, and generally puttered around looking official.

"You say somebody murdered this woman, Miss Megan?" I don't know why everybody over fifty calls her Miss Megan.

"Nicotine poisoning, Uncle Charley," said Megan. He wasn't her real uncle. Megan didn't have any uncles. She didn't have any aunts either, or cousins. Only her mother—which I guess is a good thing. It depends on which side of a cause you stand whether or not you approve of Megan's mother at any particular time. I don't imagine many people think of her as being a mother at all. She's not the sort of woman one associates with diapers and bottles and PTA meetings, although as I remember, she was president every year Megan attended school. But Megan's mom was not, and is not, a warm and fuzzy person, so I think various of her cohorts in political activism adopted Megan as a niece, a granddaughter, a daughter, or a sister to give her a sense of family.

"Now who all would want to kill this woman like that?" asked Uncle Charley.

"Just about everyone in the room."

"Is that so? Bad woman, was she?"

"Not exactly, Uncle Charley. She was more

wicked than bad." I stared at Megan. I thought the two words were synonymous.

Apparently her "Uncle Charley" understood exactly what she meant. "I see. Well, in my experience, it's wicked women who get done in faster than bad women. Bad women just mostly get beat up. But a wicked woman . . ." His voice trailed off and he rubbed his gray, handlebar mustache while he studied Jerry Carr. "That's gonna make it hard on the lieutenant here to find the guilty party. A wicked woman generally has lots of folks who wish her ill, like this one here done. You got any ideas that might help the lieutenant, Miss Megan, you better trot them out. He's gonna need a lot of help."

Clearly, the lieutenant had heard enough. "Just a minute, Charley," he interjected. "Megan Clark is a civilian. She's sort of a suspect in a previous case, and she's got as much reason to kill Denise LeClerc as anyone in this room. I can't let her help with the investigation."

Uncle Charley smoothed his mustache while he looked at the body, at Megan, at me, and finally at Jerry Carr. "That previous case would be the strangling I came out here on a couple days ago?"

"That's right. We must have missed each other."

"Everybody said Miss Megan sat with the body until you got here. I was late 'cause I was out at my place near Claude, and it took a while to get back. Takes a lot of courage to keep a dead man company. Don't hardly take any at all to murder a man, so you're caught between a rock and a hard place, ain't you, Lieutenant? You got to decide if Miss Megan's got a lot of courage, or not much at all. Not a hard choice as I see it. How about you?"

"Charley, I can't let a civilian interfere in an official investigation."

"Miss Megan is a smart woman who comes from a line of smart women, and I'd be paying attention to what she said if I was you. 'Course I'm not you. I got more sense."

He hugged Megan and kissed her cheek, nodded to me, and shuffled off the podium and toward the door. "The body's yours, Lieutenant, and you remember what I said," he called back over his shoulder as he pushed open the door and let it shut behind him.

By this time the room was empty except for Jerry and Special Crimes, Megan and me, Dr. Moser, who sat on a chair looking totally exhausted, John Harper, Reverend Robert Wilson, Dr. Yahara and David Owen Lister, and all the members of the Murder by the Yard except Agnes, who was tending her book booth.

And Denise.

"All the usual suspects, I see," said Jerry, rubbing his temples like he had another headache.

We all waited in the Apache Door Hospitality Room like refugees from a third-world country. Periodically, Jerry's henchwoman, whose name was Libby Graves I learned later, would come to the door and tell another person that "Lieutenant Carr is waiting for you," as if we were all consulting a doctor whose specialty took twenty-six letters to spell. I'm sure there must be some psychological reason for hench-woman Libby Graves to phrase the demand that one come be interrogated as an invitation to see the lieu-tenant, but I can't imagine what it is. We were being questioned by the police about a murder and we all knew it. We, meaning me, Megan, and Murder by the Yard were involved in another murder, the third in less than four months. If you think about it, you wouldn't want to invite any of us home to dinner. The percentages in favor of one of your other dinner guests keeling over in his Caesar salad, dead from poisoned croutons, are pretty good if anyone from Murder by the Yard is sitting next to him. The only good thing to be said about our propensity to attract murder is that none of our members have been vic-tims—if you discount the case last spring, and I do. That person wasn't sincere about being a member.

One by one we were called into the Yucca Room, to sit across the banquet table from Jerry Carr and henchwoman Libby Graves and answer questions, while we were recorded and videotaped. If it weren't for the honor, I could have skipped the whole thing. But that wasn't an option.

"So, Dr. Stevens, do you smoke?" asked Jerry.

"No. Raising four kids on a professor's salary didn't leave much money for vice."

"Who did you see handle the coffee and the cups?"

"You were sitting by me. It seems to me we prob-ably saw the same thing, not that there was anything unusual to see. The kid, the waiter—they all look like kids—from the restaurant brought in the urn of coffee and three insulated carafes. Megan signed a ticket as chairwoman of the convention, and Dr. Yahara filled a carafe from the urn and carried it to the podium. Dr. Moser pushed the three cups to the front of the banquet table that was sitting on the podium, and Dr. Yahara poured coffee. Afterward, Dr. Moser slid the cup on the right to John Harper, the cup on the left to Denise, and took the middle one for himself. All drank from their cups, and Denise dies. I didn't see anyone pour poison in Denise's cup. I don't see how anyone would have an opportunity to do so. I mean, with fifty people watching, at least one would have noticed and said, 'So-and-so poured something in Denise's coffee.' Wouldn't you think so, Jerry?"

Jerry drew squares, then squares within squares, on his yellow notepad, until a whole page looked like a checkerboard. Drawing squares. I always suspected he was a little too anal-retentive to ever make Megan happy.

"Did you see Dr. Moser touch Dr. LeClerc's coffee in any way? For instance, did you see him stir it?"

"No, I did not see Dr. Moser stir Denise's coffee. I did not see John Harper stir Denise's coffee. Why would anybody else stir Denise's coffee when Denise stirred it herself?" Then I suddenly saw the light, and wondered why Megan had not seen it, too. "The cream," I whispered. "The poison was in the coffee cream."

Jerry Carr's face tightened ever so slightly. If I hadn't been watching for it, I wouldn't have seen it, but, remember, I said before that Jerry's skin drew up when he was worried.

"Did you see John Harper touch the saucer with the containers of cream?" he asked.

"John was sitting to Dr. Moser's right, while Denise was sitting on his left. Why would John be passing the cream in front of Dr. Moser? John's an educated young man, and I'm sure he has better table manners than that." It was too late to take back my words when I realized the implications of what I had said.

"Did you see Dr. Moser touch the cream in any way?"

I leaned back in my chair and studied the ceiling. Megan says I always study the ceiling when I'm puzzled or thinking things through before voicing an opinion. I also look at the ceiling when I don't want to answer a question, but as I said before, not answering is not an option with Special Crimes unless you want to hire a lawyer. As far as I could tell, I wasn't a suspect in either murder nor likely to be, and I didn't need a lawyer to advise me against lying. Maybe if it had been Megan I was giving up, I would have lied anyway, or given Bill Clinton's famous "I don't recall," but it wasn't.

"I saw Dr. Moser push the saucerful of cream containers over to Denise. But I didn't see him touch any of the containers. They were the round white kind with the little tab, so you can peel off the top.

Denise would have noticed if the top of one had been loose. Wouldn't she?"

"Did you see anyone take the empty container of cream while we were making our way toward the podium?"

"You mean the container disappeared?" I asked, finally putting all the pieces together. "But how could that happen? We were all searched before you sent us to the hospitality room. No, that's not right. We weren't all searched, just the ones you called the 'usual suspects.' With the whole audience milling around the podium when Denise slid off her chair, anyone could have taken that container. Anyone could have poisoned the cream, too, because members of the audience went up to talk to the presenters between demonstrations. But how did the poisoner know that Denise would get the container, or did he or she not care which of the three died?"

"Denise is the only one who took cream in her coffee," said Jerry, acting very reluctant to share any information, but as I saw it, he had very little choice. One of us at the convention was guilty, but without the help from the rest of us, a killer would walk, because Megan was right: someone was very good at murder.

The door at the back of the room slammed open. "Lieutenant, we found the container!"

The lieutenant and his henchwoman, Libby Graves, ran for the door. "You're excused, Dr. Stevens. Get out of here."

I got out. I ever so casually, ever so silently

slouched along behind Jerry and the rest of Special Crimes, who were so excited about finding the container that they never noticed me. That's how I saw the container before anyone realized I was in the crowd.

15

*If a thing could only have been done one way, and
if only one person could have done it that way, then
you've got your criminal, motive or no motive.*

—LORD PETER WIMSEY, in Dorothy Sayers's
Busman's Honeymoon, 1937

Megan sat in one of the hospitality room's upstairs bedrooms holding Dr. Moser's hand
while he rested on the bed, two pillows elevating his
head. Members of Murder by the Yard as well as
John Harper, the Reverend Wilson, David Owen Lister, and Dr. Yahara crowded around the bed whispering. In Megan's opinion, the whole bunch
sounded like a hive of bees buzzing over a particularly succulent comb of honey, and anyone looking
less succulent than Dr. Moser she hadn't seen since
the last mummy she dissected while working on her
doctoral dissertation, and her professor came down
with an intestinal disorder, probably from drinking
the native beer the night before. It was a stressful
dissection because the professor kept screaming directions at her from his seat in the latrine. Sometimes,
when she was blue and wondering if she would ever
get a job in her profession, she thought he approved

her dissertation as a bribe to never mention his embarrassing intestinal lapse, which, however, didn't stop him from adding his name to the paper Megan wrote on the dissection. She thought that was a bit dodgy of him, so she sent him a case of the native brew along with a note saying "Wasn't our paper wonderful?" She heard later he missed a week of classes.

Dr. Moser's complexion was gray, while the mummy's had been a chocolate brown, but he looked just as shrunken and ancient. "Would you like me to call your son, Dr. Moser?" Megan asked.

The old man smiled. "Good heavens, what for? He's an old man on the edge of retirement, and if the truth were known, he has more ailments than I do. Don't worry, Miss Megan—you don't mind if I call you that?—I'll survive this latest round of life's unpleasant challenges, although I hope I'm never searched again. It is an intrusive procedure, but at least the lieutenant allowed me to sit down a few moments to gather my resources before I left. Since I supposed the police would be searching my room, I came up here to answer a call of nature and stretch out. Just a little rest and I'll be up and about again. I'm not ready to meet the Grim Reaper."

Just then Ryan flung open the bedroom door, the doorknob swiping Randal Anderson across the buttocks. "Megan! The police . . . !"

"Would you watch what the devil you're doing, Stevens!" exclaimed Randal, rubbing his right hip.

"I'm going to have a bruise the size of a grapefruit where that doorknob hit me."

"Oh, Randal," said Candi. "Do you think you broke anything? Can you walk?"

"I'll try, but you may need to help me."

"Sorry, Randal. Megan, the police—" Ryan began again.

"And that brings up a good point, Randal," said Megan, grateful that Randal didn't make a humorous remark in reply to Candi's question. She wasn't in the mood for humorous remarks. "There are just too many people in this room. Poor Dr. Moser can't rest with all of us milling around like a herd of cattle. Out, everybody. Ryan, get out of the way. You're standing in the doorway. Come over here and take Dr. Moser's pulse. I'm not sure I'm getting a correct reading."

"But, Dr. Megan Clark," protested Dr. Yahara. "I need advice. The police will accuse me of poisoning that woman."

"They won't dare, because I was watching you pour the coffee, and you did not add anything to it," said Megan.

"Megan, that's what I'm trying . . ."

"Ryan! Will you come over and take Dr. Moser's pulse? I may need to call a doctor, and I want another person to take his vitals."

"But Dr. Megan Clark, I smoke cigarettes—many cigarettes. I am what you call a chain smoker. The police will say I have the weapon." Dr. Yahara was all but wringing his hands with anxiety.

"Don't worry, Tomoyuki; I smoke cigars by the box," said Dr. Moser. "My doctor keeps telling me to quit, that smoking is bad for my health, but I tell him at my age, everything is bad for my health. If the police suspect you have the means to make the weapon, they'll have to say the same thing about me. I doubt that lieutenant will suspect us two oldsters of brewing up poison out of our smokes."

"See, Dr. Yahara, you have nothing to worry about," said Megan, as she began to physically guide people through the door.

"But that's a good point the doc makes," said Randal. "Herb and I smoke an occasional cigar."

"Oh, not often, Megan," said Call Me Herb on the heels of Randal's confession. "On birthdays and if one of the youngsters in our law firm receives a promotion to pardner. Nothing that makes me a real smoker."

"What about me?" asked David Owen Lister. "I'm a chain smoker like Dr. Yahara, and I'm not apologizing for it. If I want to smoke, I will. It's not against the law, yet. But I didn't make any poison out of my cigarettes. I wouldn't know how to do it anyway. But the cops are gonna land on me. I'm not a professor like most of the rest of you. I'm just a nobody trying to make a living on the Internet, and you know how suspicious some people are of the Internet."

"David! I didn't see you close to the table, and you certainly didn't touch the coffee cups, so relax. I'll tell Jerry that you had no opportunity to poison

Dr. LeClerc," said Megan. "So go downstairs, call the management, and tell them to please send someone to man the bar in the hospitality room. You all have plenty of drink tickets left, don't you?"

"Megan, that's what I need to tell you—" began Ryan.

"Dr. Clark, I feel I ought to tell you that I smoke an occasional pipe," said the Reverend Wilson. "I even have a can of smoking tobacco in my room. I'm sure the police will be interested in that, don't you? I would hate to be a murder suspect. It would set a bad example for my flock, and my bishop wouldn't much like it either. The only consolation I have is that missionaries to the Northern Territories are hard to find, so the bishop wouldn't call me home in disgrace."

"Reverend Wilson, I didn't see you leave your seat until the very end, when Denise had fallen out of her chair, so I hardly think Jerry would suspect you of poisoning the coffee," said Megan, guiding a limping Randal Anderson, who had his arm around a very concerned Candi Hobbs. Leave it to Randal to make the most of being hit by a doorknob, Megan thought as she watched Candi help him maneuver down the stairs.

"John!" said Megan as the young anthropologist was walking through the door after David. "You don't smoke, do you?"

John came back into the room, leaned over, and whispered in Megan's ear. He blushed and raised his head, as though even the most innocent contact with her constituted a pass. "The police won't like that, will they? I mean, it's just there and ready to turn into a weapon."

Megan patted his shoulder, thinking he was the last person in the world she would suspect of using snuff. He just didn't look the type. "Don't worry, John. We all have access to tobacco products."

"That's true, young man," said Rosemary. "Motive, means, and opportunity, those are the three legs upon which criminal investigation stands. We all have motive—Dr. LeClerc went out of her way to insult us all—we all have means whether we smoke or not. My goodness, I could buy all manner of tobacco products in the motel gift shop, and Lorene and I don't smoke at all. Dr. Stevens and Megan could buy tobacco, too, so don't worry about that. As for opportunity, I didn't see you touch Dr. LeClerc's cup, and I have very sharp eyes for my age. Lorene, did you see Mr. Harper messing about with Dr. LeClerc's cup?"

Lorene shook her head. "No, I didn't, and I have sharp eyes, too. The elderly are farsighted you know, and Rosemary and I were sitting toward the back of the room, where our sight is a real advantage. You just run on downstairs and have a drink of whatever you like, and don't worry. You have Rosemary and me on your side."

"I drink Scotch," said Harper, looking a little dazed at the way the Twins had taken up his cause. Megan didn't think it necessary to tell him it was because he reminded them of their grandsons.

Rosemary tucked her arm through his. "You know, I like a Scotch every now and then myself. Let me buy you a drink, young man."

Megan watched the Steel Mesquites lead Harper through the door.

"Finally!" she exclaimed as she locked the door. "I thought I would never get everyone out of here before you spilled whatever beans you're carrying, Ryan. I didn't want everyone to know whatever you learned because it's become obvious to me that we have to solve this crime ourselves. Now, what's eating you up?"

"I wondered why you keep interrupting me," said Ryan.

"I'm glad you're such a gentleman and didn't just shout to be heard. Now, what did you find out?"

"The police found the container in which the poison was prepared. It's a small metal cup etched with a map of Texas, with a star for Amarillo. It's a souvenir, Megan, you can buy one in the motel gift shop, the restaurants close to the motel, several places in the mall—if anyone went to the mall. I guess Jerry will be checking out all the places where they're sold to see if anyone remembers selling one to any of us."

"Where did they find the cup, Ryan?"

"In a Dempster Dumpster back of the motel. Someone had just thrown it on top of the other trash, didn't even make an attempt to bury it where it wouldn't be seen. I don't understand that—unless the murderer thinks the cup can't be traced. There are no fingerprints, I know that. I heard one of the techs say so before Jerry caught me and told me to, well, beat it, not exactly in those words. The longer this investigation lasts, the more profane Jerry's language becomes."

"That's understandable, Dr. Stevens," said Dr. Moser, raising his head off the pillow. "Lieutenant Carr is frustrated because his investigation is stalled. Perhaps finding this cup will give it new impetus." Exhausted, he let his head fall back to his pillow.

"How did Jerry know the cup was used to prepare the poison?" asked Megan.

"It was coated with a sticky syrup that smelled like tobacco. I saw Jerry bend down and sniff it, and say, 'That's it. Stinks like tobacco.' "

Megan paced the small bedroom nibbling her thumbnail while Dr. Moser and Ryan watched her. Finally, she stopped and collapsed into a chair in the corner by the bed. "So we know what the poison was prepared in, but we still don't know how it was administered. I mean, how did it get into Denise's cup when the coffee was poured into all three cups from the same carafe?"

"The cream," announced Ryan. "That's the other thing I've been trying to tell you. Denise was the only one of the three who took cream in her coffee, so the cream at the podium was poisoned. Denise poured it into her coffee, drank, and she was kaput."

"The cream," said Megan, sitting up straight. "I never thought of the coffee cream. That changes everything. Anyone could have poisoned the cream at any time during the demonstrations, knowing that sooner or later Denise would pick up the container with the poisoned cream. She could have died anytime this afternoon. The killer didn't even have to be present. How did Jerry figure out the poison was in the cream, Ryan? Did he smell it?"

"I think he used a process of elimination. The container has disappeared and the coffee cup hasn't," said Ryan.

"The container has disappeared?" repeated Megan. "But where did it go? It wasn't on the floor of the podium or underneath the table, so it didn't fall by accident. But how did somebody remove it from the room when we were all searched? And all our purses, sacks, briefcases, everything was searched but our underwear and Jerry would have searched there if he thought he could get away with it. I imagine he didn't know at that point that the cream containers were important, but anyone searching us would notice a cream container in our pockets or in our belongings and recognize it as an anomaly. I mean, how many people save their empty cream containers?"

"Isn't there a possibility that the lieutenant is mistaken?" asked Dr. Moser. "Maybe the poison was already in her cup before Tomoyuki poured the coffee?"

"I suppose there's a chance of that being the case," said Megan. "But surely he would have noticed that there was an oily substance in her cup."

"Tomoyuki is Japanese, Megan, and as a member of that ethic group, he is rather short compared with the average American. I doubt he could see the bottom of her cup, since he was standing on the floor in front of the podium," said Dr. Moser. "I wouldn't mention that possibility to him, though, because he would first of all be offended, and second, he would feel that he played a role in her death, all because he was too short to see the bottom of her coffee cup. He's a very gentle man and has been a lifelong friend of mine. I would not like to see him distressed."

"That the poison was already in her cup is a possibility I hadn't considered, Dr. Moser. But again there is the problem of when it was added to her cup. I'm not even sure what constitutes a lethal dose of nicotine without looking it up in a toxicology text, so I don't know how much would have to be added, but I would think Denise would notice if anyone poured a little something extra in her coffee cup." Megan paced again from bed to door and back again.

"I wish you would perch somewhere," said Ryan. "I'm getting a sore neck from trying to follow you. I turn my head less watching a tennis match."

"I think better when I walk, and what I'm thinking now is that we had better cross off our list anyone adding anything to Denise's cup. I don't think it's feasible. Too many pairs of eyes watching. The risk was unacceptable to the murderer."

"What list?" ask Ryan. "I get nervous when you start talking about lists, because it makes me think you're messing around in a police investigation again. I told you because I thought we might figure out how the poison was added to the cream and tell Jerry Carr. He could take it from there. He figured out the cream part, didn't he, Megan? Don't you think we can trust him with the rest of the investigation."

"If I had trusted him with the last investigation you didn't want me involved in, my first-degree-murder case would be coming up on the court docket about now," said Megan. "So pardon me if I don't have the confidence in Jerry Carr that you do."

"He seems to be doing a good job so far," said Ryan, his brows drawing together, always a sign that he was losing patience.

When Megan and Ryan's oldest daughter, Evin, were growing up, Megan always gaged just how far they could push Ryan by how close together his eyebrows were. When she was a child, Ryan would send her home when he finally lost patience. Now that she was grown, he got stubborn as an old mule instead.

"Ryan, please, I don't have time to argue you into helping me. We're running out of time. The banquet is tonight, and tomorrow Jerry will have to let everyone go home—or arrest them—and I don't think he has the necessary evidence to arrest anyone. I know that Brownleigh and Denise were both pond scum when it came to character, but I don't like the idea of anyone killing them, and I especially don't like the idea of someone killing them at MY convention."

"That's all the more reason to help Jerry Carr, Megan. We have no power to arrest people, or force them to stay in town. We're—we're civilians, just like Jerry said, and we didn't even figure out that the poison was in the cream, so how can we solve this murder?" Ryan was so sincere that he was sweating.

"By going to the source, Ryan—the victims. I wish I had gotten a closer look at Denise's body. As it was, the only thing I can say with any confidence is that she didn't smoke and she was probably diabetic."

"How the devil do you know she was diabetic? Did you see her shoot up her insulin?" asked Ryan, his eyebrows crawling close together again. "I didn't see a medic alert bracelet on her arm."

"She wasn't wearing a medic alert—which means she probably carries a card in her billfold. As for seeing her shoot up, as you put it, diabetics most commonly inject their insulin in the area of the navel, or the thighs, and I could hardly whip up Denise's blouse or skirt to check for any injection marks with half the Western world standing around and gawking. The dead deserve some privacy. But I noticed tiny puncture marks on the tips of two of her fingers, where she apparently had to pierce herself more than once at the same time. A simple magnifying glass would have probably revealed puncture marks on the other fingers, but where is Sherlock Holmes when you really need him?"

"Sherlock Holmes is a fictional character," said Ryan.

Megan patted his arm. "Never mind, Ryan. I always forget that you're humor-challenged when it comes to mystery fiction."

"I got the connection—Sherlock Holmes and his magnifying glass—but I don't understand the significance of the puncture marks as a clue that Denise was a diabetic," said Ryan, sounding a little snappish. He was always on the defensive when it came to the world of mystery fiction, about which he knew enough to put in the proverbial thimble.

"Diabetics test their blood-sugar levels several times a day by squeezing a drop of blood, usually from a fingertip, touching it to a test strip whose capillary action draws the blood into the reaction chamber in a handheld machine, which provides the diabetic with a digital readout of his glucose level." Megan shrugged her shoulders, trying to appear casual. "At least, that's how my mother does it."

"I didn't know your mother was diabetic," said Ryan.

"Since last year. It's why she's not so much into causes now. She has to conserve her energy. She'll be amused to hear that her diabetes was good for something, even if it is so minor as my being able to make the connection between puncture marks on Denise's fingertips and a physical disease. Mom's been bitter about this whole diabetic thing."

"Your mother has my sympathy," said Dr. Moser. "As you get older you have a take a pill to replace every enzyme, fluid, or hormone the body used to make for itself. I have enough pill bottles to build a retaining wall across the Mississippi River Valley. Whoever called these the golden years was referring to the amount of money we spend on prescription drugs."

"Let's tell Jerry Carr that Denise was a diabetic,

and let him figure out how it fits in with her murder—if it does," said Ryan.

"All right, I'll go tell him. Maybe then he'll figure
out how the poison got in the cream."

"Wait a minute, Megan. How *did* the poison get
into the cream?" asked Ryan.

"Simple. A needle," she replied as she unlocked
the door and walked out.

She found Jerry Carr in back of the motel super-
vising a search of the Dempster Dumpster and the
surrounding parking lot. "Jerry, I think I know how
the poison got in the cream."

"How?" he asked without looking at her.

"A needle."

He glanced down at her. "At least we agree on
something. Doc Stevens pointed out that if the top of
the cream container was loose, then Denise would
have noticed it. I started thinking of other ways to
get something inside a closed container without taking off the lid. A hypodermic needle is the obvious
solution. Jab it through the thin foil lid, leaving a
minuscule hole that LeClerc probably didn't notice,
and you've got your poisoned cream."

"But you can't prove it because you don't have the
container."

"Something else we agree on." He looked back at
his techs in their white hazard uniforms digging
through the Dumpster with all the enthusiasm of kids
contemplating a serving of spinach.

"I need to know a few other facts before I can
formulate a workable theory for the murder," said

Megan, pleased that she and Jerry seemed to be on the same page for once. "I need to know whose fingerprints you found in Denise's room, what the search turned up, and if she was insulin-dependent."

That brought Jerry whirling to face her. He put his hands on her shoulders and squeezed gently, then turned her around and pushed her toward the motel's back door. "Butt out, Megan. Special Crimes has this under control, and you're not a member of Special Crimes. Let me do my job without someone looking over my shoulder second-guessing me. It's gets to be disconcerting. And tell the rest of your amateur sleuths to restrict their sleuthing to playing a game of Clue. Otherwise, *your* meddling will get them all killed."

Megan paused at the back door, debating whether to tell Jerry Carr that not only was he a jerk, he was a stupid jerk, but her eyes were blurry with tears, and she had vowed long ago never to let a man see her cry—except maybe Ryan Stevens under very special circumstances, like if her dog died or she broke an arm. How dare he accuse her of putting her friends in danger. No . . . Jerry was wrong. Murder by the Yard's involvement would prevent more murders. They could solve this one, just like that case last spring.

She wiped her nose and eyes on her T-shirt and walked into the motel and straight to Agnes's book booth. "Agnes, close your booth. I'm calling a meeting of Murder by the Yard at the bookstore. Pass the word."

Agnes didn't argue, but grabbed a box and started packing books. Megan walked across the open square to the Sagebrush Room, slipped inside through the double doors at the front, and walked out through the service door in the back. Just as she had suspected, Jerry had not thought to assign a guard to the Yucca Room's service door. Glancing up and down the service hall and seeing nobody, she took a credit card out of her billfold and inserted it between the door-jamb and the lock. She heard the satisfying click then opened the door an inch at a time until she saw that the Yucca Room was empty. She slipped inside and went immediately to the banquet table. The inventory list of Denise's room and her personal belongings was on the top of a stack of other papers. She nudged it apart and read the inventory, glad that her memory, if not photographic, ran a close second. Within five minutes she had finished reading and slipped back out the service door unseen.

16

THE CIRCLE

A figure from the Inuit of Cumberland Sound,
Baffin Land; p. 127 of *String Figures and How
to Make Them* by Caroline Furness Jayne.

1. First Position.

2. Insert R2, R3, R4, and R5 (Right Index, Middle, Ring, and Little Fingers) from below behind the L Palmar (string across Left Palm) string and return. Repeat with Left Hand.

3. Release 1 Loops (Thumb Loops) and pick up 5n with 1 (Pick Up near string on Little Fingers with Right and Left Thumbs) and return.

3a. Perform the movement of Opening A.

4. With the opposite hand, remove each hand loop in turn and drop them into the middle of the figure.

5. Extend slowly and a circle will appear.

Megan and I drove our separate trucks to the Time and Again Bookstore on Sixth Street as a precaution against another argument. She and I seldom argue, and we were both tired of the sharp words we'd exchanged about what the newspapers later called the Case of Cheating the Hangman. I don't know why Megan persists in conducting a parallel investigation with Special Crimes. Jerry Carr hadn't done too badly on this case. Not like last spring, when he wasn't all that sharp on deducing what had really happened and why. But Megan was convinced that Jerry would never catch the murderer, and that she could. I can't argue her out of interfering, so I might as well go along to keep her out of as much trouble as possible. What other choice do I have?

It was close to five o'clock when I drove down Sixth Street, that quiet hour when the tourists with armloads of antiques have gone and the local Amarilloans haven't yet ventured down to the restaurants and dance clubs and spilled outside to stand on the sidewalks or loll on the park benches. The petunias were profusely blooming in the clay flowerpots that stood near the door to every business, and the trees, many of which were also planted in clay pots, were casting what shade they could, given their young age and size. The Victorian-looking streetlights, black wrought-iron poles and round white globes, wouldn't come on until after eight this time of year, maybe later than that, so the late-afternoon light would have no rival. I always felt a sense of history driving down Sixth Street, a connection with those worn-out old cars and pickups of the thirties, carrying tens of thousands of Okies, and Texies, and Arkies, whose only hope was a dream of better times in a magic land by the ocean. I usually felt at peace, too, as I do at any historical site.

Not today, however, not with Megan Clark on a tear, and waiting for me at Time and Again Bookstore near the end of Sixth Street.

I pulled into the parking lot and dawdled as long as I dared, looking at the panoramic scenes painted on the one blank wall that was the long leg of the L-shaped bookstore. The short leg faced the street, with one window displaying the latest in new and used books, usually mysteries and Westerns and the occasional romance, and contained a tall, black double wooden door that was the entrance. On the wall next to the door is painted a grandfather clock with "Time and Again Bookstore" printed in a half circle above it. The long leg of the L shape held extra display space, storage rooms, and Agnes's two-bedroom apartment.

The bookstore's front door was locked, so I knocked.

"Who's there?" asked Agnes, her voice muffled by the thick, solid wood door.

"Come on, Agnes, you know who it is."

"Give me your personal password."

"Watson," I said, thinking that the members of the Murder by the Yard Reading Circle spend way too much time reading mystery-and-suspense fiction and watching Mel Gibson videos.

Agnes unlocked the door and I walked in. Megan was already there, sitting on the couch in the reading area and tapping one foot. She looked a little pale, with reddened eyes and a somber face. I suddenly felt sorry I had argued with her. Megan Clark would do what her personality and character called her to do, and nothing anyone said or did would make a difference.

"I know you think these passwords are just part of a game that a bunch of silly adults play with no lives outside of Murder by the Yard, but it's a harmless game, Ryan, and what is wrong with harmless games if they bring enjoyment?" asked Agnes, locking the door behind me.

"Plenty, if we want to do five to ten."

"Oh, is that what the sentence is for interfering with a police investigation?" asked Agnes.

"I don't know!" I exclaimed. "But I do know that we're on the narrow edge of committing an illegal act."

Megan rose and clasped her hands, holding them together at her waist like some religious acolyte. She met my eyes and I couldn't break away. "Clyde Brownleigh died a premature death by violence. He wasn't a particularly worthy human being in my opinion, but he didn't deserve to be strangled."

The members of Murder by the Yard were silent and still, like primitive worshipers at some stone altar, their eyes on Megan, intense expressions on their faces, as if they were afraid to look away for fear of missing some important part of a ceremony. What was worse was the way I stood at the edge of the little reading area directly opposite Megan, as though I, too, was part of the rite.

"Denise LeClerc died a premature death by violence. She also was not a worthy human being. Furthermore, I referred to her as a wicked woman this morning, and I believe she was. Denise LeClerc deliberately tried to arouse suspicion in Jerry Carr's mind against Candi Hobbs. She succeeded to the extent that Candi was read her rights, the so-called Miranda rights, and became an official suspect in Clyde Brownleigh's murder."

Megan paused, finally looking away from me to Candi Hobbs, plain little Candi, who I would be willing to bet never committed a criminal act of any kind in her life, including speeding.

"Yet Candi Hobbs is not guilty of anything but defending herself against cruel and petty remarks by Denise LeClerc," continued Megan. She paused and looked back at me. I took a step toward her, then stopped.

"Denise LeClerc deliberately lied about seeing me sneak out of Clyde Brownleigh's room at one o'clock the night he was murdered. I was there at twelve-thirty, not at one."

Herb Jackson sighed. "You've made us all witnesses, Megan. If Jerry Carr should ask us, we would have to testify as to what you just said. If I were your attorney instead of Candi's, I would have advised you not to say anything, particularly about being in Brownleigh's room."

Megan didn't spare a glance for Herb. It was as though she was explaining her thoughts and conduct to me, and members of Murder by the Yard were there only to bear witness, not interrupt with their own thoughts. I began to sense for the first time that Megan already had planned what actions she intended to take, and if we chose to support her, we could, but she would not demand it, might not even ask for it.

I felt chills crawl up and down my spine.

"Yet I did not murder Clyde Brownleigh, and Jerry Carr does not seriously believe that I did. But Denise LeClerc saw someone going in or leaving Clyde Brownleigh's room at one A.M., which is about the time of his death. When he opened his door to that second visitor after the official appointments ended, he opened his door to Death. Dr. Yahara said that Brownleigh may have earned his death, that his murder, far from disrupting society, actually restored order to it, because his actions in selling the Jayne manuscript were criminal. That is the sort of philosophy to be discussed at a cocktail party that T. S. Eliot might write about. I will have none of it. Some among us may ask to be murdered by our individual acts, but it is not the right of any of us to commit murder."

Those chills were now racing up and down my spine, and I had taken another step closer to Megan, standing alone in front of the couch.

"Jerry Carr"—she paused and bit her lip, and I knew he had hurt her—"Jerry Carr refuses to use my expertise, so I'll uncover the murderer myself, and the first question I'll ask is what's the motive for Denise's murder—other than foul temper, and that's not a good enough reason. Otherwise, at least a quarter of the earth's population would be murdered."

"It's obvious," said Randal Anderson. "She was murdered by whoever she saw at one A.M."

"How did the murderer know that he had been seen?" asked Megan.

There was silence, which I broke, much to my own surprise. "Denise intimated to me that she had seen someone else at Brownleigh's door at one o'clock, but we were sitting together on the couch and she was whispering in my ear at the time, so I don't think anyone heard. And I never told anyone but Megan."

"And she told all of us," said Rosemary. "But I didn't tell any strangers, and didn't talk about it to anyone but Lorene and Agnes."

"And I certainly didn't flap my jaws to anyone," said Agnes. "And I don't imagine that Lorene did."

"I didn't," said Lorene, shaking her head. "I was afraid that Megan might get into more trouble if anyone else but us knew about it."

"I know the answer!" said Herb.

"It's not necessary to hold up your hand, Herb," said Megan. "Just tell us."

"When you took the note to the podium, everyone in the room could overhear Denise, and she said something about seeing someone loitering in the hall outside Brownleigh's room."

"That was already too late, Herb. The coffee cream had already been poisoned."

"The coffee cream!" exclaimed Rosemary. "This

is the most interesting poisoning case since *A Pale Horse* by dear Agatha Christie."

"I would disagree, Rosemary," said Lorene. "I find that *Strong Poison* by Dorothy Sayers is a more classical case of poisoning."

"That's the difficulty with it. *Strong Poison* is so very classical, while *A Pale Horse* breaks new ground in the genre," argued Rosemary.

"Ladies! Please, this is not a mystery discussion," I said. Let those two loose on the novels by Christie and Sayers, and we would be here until the middle of next year.

"We're so sorry, Ryan. We were getting off the subject. But it seems that nobody told anyone outside this reading circle about Denise's witnessing a man outside Brownleigh's room."

"Why do you think it's a man?" Candi asked.

"Rosemary's right, it was a man that Denise saw."

Most of the membership, including me, jerked or twitched. I think we had forgotten the high priestess standing in front of the couch. I never envisioned a priestess in hiking boots, T-shirt, and carpenter's pants, but it's a new millennium.

"If we are all innocent of Clyde's murder, and I believe we are, then we are all innocent of Denise's murder. That leaves the rest of what Jerry Carr called the 'usual suspects'—Dr. Yahara, Dr. Moser, Reverend Robert Wilson, David Owen Lister, and John Harper. Outside of Rosemary and Herb Jackson, they were the only individuals who bid on the Jayne manuscript, so I think we can safely point at one of them as the murderer."

"Which one did the dastardly deeds, Megan?" asked Randal. Leave it to Randal to couch his question in such a melodramatic manner. I could almost see a villain in a black cape tying the sweet young thing to the railroad tracks.

"I don't know, but I do know the mechanisms of the murder."

I wasn't sure what she was talking about.

"Keeping in mind the advice you gave me, Herb, and also keeping in mind that you are an officer of the court, and thus obligated to turn in an individual for an illegal act, let me just say that—"

"Wait!" yelled Herb. "Don't say anything for a moment. Candi, in view of the fact you are no longer a suspect in the Brownleigh case, because you are most certainly not a suspect in the LeClerc murder, and the two are connected, I believe that you can release me as your attorney so that Megan can hire me. Or I can go to the men's room so I won't hear anything Megan has to say."

Clearly, the men's room was becoming a popular refuge.

"Herb, you can't let Candi fire you because everyone in this room is still a viable suspect for Denise's murder," said Megan, looking more somber and alone by the minute.

I couldn't let her stand up there by herself. I walked across the reading area and swept her up in a hug, whirling her around like the model in one of those shampoo commercials on TV. I felt her trembling and knew that however tough and strong Megan Clark was, she was close to the end of her strength. "It's all right, honey, I'm with you all the way, even if it means spending quality time with Guido, the three-hundred-pound biker, as my cell mate."

I heard her giggle.

Then I heard the applause. I opened my eyes and lifted my face out of the curve of Megan's neck, and saw Murder by the Yard giving us a standing O.

I let Megan down until her hiking boots touched the floor, took her by the hand, and we bowed to our friends. Silly, serious, caring, sarcastic, boring, loving, sensible, all the adjectives you can think of that describe the human condition fit the Murder by the Yard Reading Circle, and they were our friends.

I stood behind Megan, close enough for her to feel my presence, but not too close to make her twitch. Megan can be a hugger sometimes, but when her mind is on business, she is very much hands-off.

"What did you mean that I'm still a viable suspect for Denise's murder?" asked Candi. "And what about Randal? Is he a suspect, too?"

"Yes, Megan, I think you need to explain your statement," said Agnes, tucking a loose strand of hair back into her bun, or whatever women call those knots of hair they wear on the backs of their heads.

"Denise did not drink poisoned coffee," began Megan, then corrected herself. "Well, she did, but it wasn't the coffee that was poisoned. It was the cream. I believe that whoever brewed up the nicotine poisoning—"

"Now that's an interesting poison," said Candi. "I believe it was first used by the Count and Countess de Bocarme to murder her brother, Gustave Fougnies, in France in 1850. At least, that's the first time the poison was isolated from the body tissues."

"Is that so?" asked Rosemary. "Agnes, do you know of a mystery in which nicotine poison was the murder weapon?"

"I can't think of one offhand, Rosemary, and that was very interesting history, Candi, but I believe we had better listen to Megan. Apparently we may all need to prepare our defenses."

"Thank you, Agnes," said Megan. "As I was saying, I believe and Jerry Carr believes—at least, I think he does—that the poison was injected into the container of cream through the lid, which is only foil. A small needle prick would hardly be noticeable."

"Is this the part where I need to go to the men's room?" asked Herb.

Megan smiled, the first one I had seen since Denise's murder. "I'll warn you in plenty of time, Herb."

"Take a folding chair and a book, Herb," I said.

"I'll take a chair, but I'll use the time to revise the last chapter of my legal thriller."

If that's what Call Me Herb planned to do, then someone would have to go wake him up after the meeting—unless his novel failed to put him to sleep the way it did the rest of us.

"Wouldn't Denise notice somebody injecting her coffee cream?" asked Randal.

"Think about the demonstrations this afternoon. After nearly every one, members of the audience, including all of us except Ryan, crowded around the podium to ask questions of the presenter. Anyone could have pocketed a container of cream, taken it back to his seat with him, and very subtly injected it with the poison. Or gone outside for a cigarette, or gone to the men's room, or stood in the hall looking out one of the windows with his back to the door of the Sagebrush Room. Then the murderer could palm the container, and drop it back in the saucer with the other containers of cream. It didn't matter when Denise opened that particular container, because the murderer didn't care when she died, just as long as she did."

"That's very clever," said Lorene. "I'm surprised that no one has thought to write a mystery using that plot."

Lorene didn't need to worry. I was already hard at work. But I was waiting for the solution myself.

"Where did the murderer get the hypodermic needle?" asked Rosemary. "I didn't think any of Jerry Carr's 'usual suspects' looked like drug addicts who would 'shoot up.' Certainly, that young John Harper is too nice to have a nasty drug habit. And drug habits are nasty, aren't they?"

"Yes, Rosemary. Drug habits are nasty and you don't meet the best kind of people on street corners selling drugs. But to get back to my theory," said Megan.

"Do I need to leave yet?" asked Herb. "Because I don't want to hear a single thing that I shouldn't."

"I'll tell you in plenty of time," said Megan, through gritted teeth.

I noticed that she was beginning to clench her fists at her sides, and knew she was running short of patience. She always clenched her fists then—and wrinkled her forehead.

"Denise was a diabetic, and diabetics usually carry a kit with them that contains a hypodermic filled with sterile water and a vial of powdered glucose, because odd as it may sound, having low blood sugar can be as dangerous to a diabetic as having blood sugar that is too high. If a diabetic is having a hypoglycemic attack, then she can mix up a syringe of glucose and inject it to bring her blood sugar up to normal levels."

Megan paused and looked at Herb. "You may go to the men's room now." She waited until Herb smoothed his vest, his T-shirt, and his Levi's, picked up his metal folding chair and his briefcase, and disappeared toward the bathrooms before she continued. "I was able to look at the inventory list of Denise's personal belongings. There was a vial of powdered glucose in a kit found in her purse, but no needle. Someone picked Denise's pocket, or purse, took the syringe, and replaced the kit. If Denise didn't have a hypoglycemic crisis, she wouldn't have missed the syringe. And believe me, if she had missed the syringe, we would have all been accused of being pickpockets."

17

*A detective who minds his own business would be
a contradiction in terms.*

—ARCHIE GOODWIN, in Rex Stout's
Some Buried Caesar, 1938

Megan could feel Ryan's presence behind her
like a tall, sun-warmed wall against which she
could lean anytime she chose. But she didn't choose.
Ryan was backup in case her nerve failed her; he was
supportive even though he disagreed with everything
she wanted to do. How strange that a member of the
baby-boomer generation, the rebellious generation,
wanted to call the cops. That she didn't would be no
surprise to anyone with the least understanding of
Generation X. Her generation was independent, self-
reliant, and distrustful of institutions, although in her
case the distrust of institutions might have been
passed along with mother's milk, or maybe it was in
her DNA.

"So what do we have? Brownleigh has the ru-
mored lost Caroline Furness Jayne manuscript which
he offers to sell to the highest bidder. Those bidding
are Rosemary and Herb from Murder by the Yard,
although all of us made appointments to see it; and

Drs. Moser, Yahara, and LeClerc, the Reverend Wilson, David Owen Lister, and John Harper. So who killed Brownleigh and stole the manuscript? Obviously, someone who wanted the manuscript very badly, and was afraid his bid was not high enough to win the auction. Who are our candidates? Would anyone care to guess?"

"My bid was not very high, as I told you, Megan," said Rosemary. "But I didn't have the passion to own it that the true string-figure enthusiasts felt. Men like Dr. Moser and Dr. Yahara—he's such a nice man, who yesterday told me the history behind the Japanese tea ceremony—and the Reverend Wilson and John Harper have such a passion for string figures. I suspect they each bid everything they owned to win that auction. David Owen Lister would not be able to compete, in my opinion, so if someone murdered Brownleigh because he couldn't afford to outbid the others, my guess would be Lister."

"I suppose before we discuss any more candidates for murderer of the year, someone ought to go tell Herb that it's safe to come out of the men's room," said Megan.

"I'll volunteer," said Randal. "I need to visit the facilities anyway."

Only Randal would think that the reading circle was interested in his toilet habits, thought Megan as she stretched. Her muscles were so tight from stress that she would be sore tomorrow, and she had Sunday-afternoon duty at the reference desk. Maybe she would have a quiet afternoon. On the other hand, she might be dead.

"I had to wake him up," said Randal, returning from the man's room and taking his seat by Candi. "He was snoring like the devil."

"I apologize," said Herb, hurrying in with his briefcase. "I was revising chapter fifteen of my book and I fell asleep. I must be more tired from the convention that I thought."

Megan smiled, thinking of the last chapter of Herb's book that she had tried to read. She fell asleep after three pages. Agnes claimed that was a record, that no one else in the reading circle had lasted more than two.

"Herb, Rosemary's candidate for the murderer of Brownleigh and by default, Denise LeClerc, is David Owen Lister," said Megan. "Do you have an alternative suggestion?"

"Before she was murdered I was sure it was LeClerc. I thought she had stolen the manuscript and that's where she got the page she put in Candi's purse. I was wrong, so my next guess is the Reverend Robert Wilson."

"Absolutely not!" exclaimed Rosemary and Lorene as one.

"He's a fine Christian gentleman," said Lorene. "I know he wanted the manuscript so very badly so the Nauru Islanders can learn the culture they lost, but a man who believes that the inhabitants of a tiny Pacific island are just as important as the inhabitants of, well, New York City, can't have murdered two people. Not when he cares about saving an art the majority of the world considers trivial, just because it's important to the Nauru Islanders. To them it isn't trivial. It's part of their history."

"He was planning to sell a piece of property that had been in his family for nearly four hundred years, so he could afford to make a generous bid," said Rosemary. "I think you're wrong, Herb."

"It's been my experience as a lawyer that religious fanatics can appear to be very rational until the issue they are fanatical over is, to their mind, threatened. I'm not saying that the Reverend Wilson is a fanatic, but he was very intense about that cultural center on Nauru Island," said Herb. "I wouldn't say that he was obsessed with it, but he comes awfully close."

"I think you're mistaking obsession with passion," said Rosemary.

Megan clapped her hands. "Okay, Rosemary and Lorene think it's David Owen Lister, and Herb votes for the reverend. Did anyone see either of those two at the demonstrations today?"

"The reverend was there the entire afternoon— well, until Denise LeClerc died," said Herb.

"I saw David Owen Lister," Lorene volunteered.

"There's no need to ask about Dr. Moser and John Harper, since they shared the podium with Denise," said Megan. "What about Dr. Yahara? He certainly was obsessed with the manuscript."

"He is a nice gentleman," said Rosemary.

"Yes, he is," agreed Lorene.

"But he poured the coffee," said Randal. "Did he also bring fresh containers of cream?"

There was silence while each member tried to remember. Megan knew that some of what the members were certain of never happened. Carrying a handful of containers of cream and adding them to a saucer already on the podium was such a mundane task that no one remembered it, but some might think they did. That was what was so frustrating about eye-witnesses. They all saw the same people committing the same acts, and they all remembered differently.

"Does anyone remember seeing one of our suspects, or anybody for that matter, fiddling with the containers of cream?" asked Megan.

Everyone shook their heads.

"Didn't the police find any fingerprints on the container?" asked Candi.

"The cream container disappeared," said Megan.

"It didn't disappear," said Randal. "The police didn't find it. There's a difference."

"Do you have any idea where it was hidden, Randal?"

"I can make a guess, and I bet Ryan can, too. Hey, Ryan, whenever a student got some contraband, or a cheat sheet, or whatever he doesn't want to be caught with, what does he do?"

Megan heard Ryan suck in a breath. "He sticks it under his chair or his desk with chewing gum."

"You got it," said Randal. "Look under all the chairs in the Sagebrush Room and you're going to find that container—that is, unless Jerry Carr has already found it. But Jerry was never a teacher. Takes a teacher who's put up with students for years to know all the tricks and to use them when he needs to. I bet you if you turn up all the chairs in the Sagebrush Room, you'll find a big glob of chewing gum and hiding inside that glob is a cream container. Let's go down there and see. The Sagebrush Room was a crime scene this afternoon, but I bet Jerry Carr's gang is through with it by now. Besides, that's where our banquet is supposed to be."

Ryan later told Megan that he had spoken her name twice before she heard him, and when she did answer, she seemed to be hearing everyone's voices from a distance. "What did you say?" she asked.

Ryan frowned as he studied her. "Are you all right?"

"Yes, I'm fine. Just a little distracted, trying to put together all the clues."

"Randal's ready to lead a charge on the chairs in the Sagebrush Room. You want to go, too, or go home and change for the banquet?"

"The container won't still be there, so I might as well go home and change clothes. My mother bought me a dress. I can hardly wait to see what it looks like. She thinks I dress like a Sicilian widow, and I think her taste in clothes for me makes me look like I'm dressed in a fruit salad."

"How do you know the container won't be there?" asked Ryan.

"Because I know how the container left the room, and why nobody noticed a thing."

"Are you telling me that you know the murder's identity?"

"Maybe. I'll know for sure after tonight." She clapped her hands several times. "I'm not done yet. I have a plan to trap the murderer."

"Wait a minute!" yelled Ryan. "What's this business about trapping a murderer? I won't have anything to do with that!"

"Then go to the men's room," said Megan. "Because my plan is the only way to reveal a murderer. Jerry Carr will never solve this crime. He has no idea how the cream container got out of the Sagebrush Room. He doesn't know why the metal cup used to prepare the nicotine poison was lying on top of the trash in the Dumpster, he doesn't know why the Jayne manuscript was stolen, and he doesn't know why Denise LeClerc wasn't afraid of a murderer— although as it turned out, she should have been."

"What is your plan, Megan?" asked Agnes. "And how can Murder by the Yard help? That *is* why you called a meeting, isn't it? To ask for our help?"

"Yes, but no one has to help if he or she feels uncomfortable. Herb, you might want to consider if you should be involved," said Megan.

"Yeah, Herb, consider how you're going to make a living after you're disbarred for trying to do a job the police can do better," said Ryan. "As for myself, maybe the prison officials will let me do a little teaching after four or five years in stir."

"In stir? My God, Ryan, where *do* you pick up these expressions?" asked Megan.

"Did I say something wrong?" he asked, bewildered again that his film noir terms were as outdated as record players.

"Never mind, Ryan. Just sit down and listen to everything I say before you start screaming. It's always hard to explain a plan while you're screaming."

"Go ahead, Megan," said Agnes. "We're raring to go."

"Tonight, while everyone is at the banquet, I will slip notes under the doors of Dr. Moser, Dr. Yahara, Reverend Wilson, David Owen Lister, and John Harper. I will claim that I have the manuscript, and am willing to sell it to the highest bidder. Beginning at midnight, I'll wait in the hospitality room with the drapes drawn. Four of these five men will come to offer me money. One will come to kill me. When that person comes, all of Murder by the Yard will rush out and confront him. He's a poisoner. He's not the type to shoot five or six people. Faced by the knowledge that we know what he did, he'll cave. I guarantee it."

"Damn, but that makes me feel confident," said Ryan in a tone of voice very close to a shout. "You guarantee it! Right! Remember the last case of murder you sleuthed around in?"

"Sleuthed?" asked Megan. "I don't think that's a proper word."

"Don't try to wiggle out of a lecture. . . ." began Ryan.

"I don't have time to be lectured, Ryan. It's nearly six and I need to go home and put on the fruit-salad dress my mother bought me, and I still have to assign hiding places."

"Hiding places?"

"Yes, you don't think the murderer will come waltzing in if the entire Murder by the Yard Reading Circle is sitting on the couches waiting, do you?" asked Megan with as much sarcasm as she could muster on a bad day.

"Oh, my God!" exclaimed Ryan, and sat down on the couch with his head buried in his hands.

"Give us our assignments," said Lorene. "And I'm going to carry a sock full of coins in my purse just in case I need to wallop him over the head. Even if it turns out to be Reverend Wilson, I'll wallop him."

"That's an excellent idea, Lorene," said Rosemary. "I think I shall do the same. In my opinion there is no better blackjack that a cotton sock full of quarters. You should always use cotton because nylon socks stretch, and you would soon end up dragging your blackjack behind you and that wouldn't be very useful."

"I'll carry a brick in my purse," said Candi. "There was a mystery set on Amarillo Boulevard in which the heroine carried a brick in her purse and let a pimp have it. Do you remember it, Agnes?"

"Yes, it was *Murder by Masquerade* and I could sell a thousand copies if I could get them, but it's out of print."

"Do you remember the author's name, Agnes?" asked Randal.

"Oh, I know it as well as my own, but it's slipped

my mind. As soon as I think of it, I'll tell you, Randal."

Megan slapped her hands again. Everyone was so easily distracted today. It must be the stress. "Randal, I want you hiding in that big bush just outside the sliding-glass door. Agnes, please hide in the coat closet by the front door. Leave it open just a bit so you can hear. Rosemary, you will hide in the pantry, and Lorene, crouch down behind that big potted plant in the corner by the bar. Herb, if you will wait upstairs in the bedroom with the door open, and Candi, behind the sofa. It's got that little flounce all around the bottom, but if you lift it up, you can slide right under. Ryan—"

"I'll figure out a place to hide when we get there, and it's going to be as close to you as I can get. And don't bother arguing with me either, because you'll lose."

18

MAN IN A BED

A figure from the Torres Straits, found on page 192 of *String Figures and How to Make Them* by Caroline Furness Jayne.

1. Opening A.

2. 1 (Right and Left Thumbs) under 2 Loops (Loops on the Right and Left Index Fingers), then into 5 Loops (Loops on Right and Left Little Finger) from below and return with 5n (near string on Right and Left Little Fingers).

3. 5 (Right and Left Little Fingers) from above, through the 2 Loops (Loops on Right and Left Index Fingers), then Pick Up (retrieve a string using the nail side of the Finger) 1f (far string on the Right and Left Thumbs), and return.

4. Release 2 Loops (the Loops on Right and Left Index Fingers).

I went home, changed clothes, and found a weapon. Unlike many Texas home owners, I don't have a plethora of guns from which to choose. Raising four children plus Megan, who spent as much

time at my house as she did at her own, I figured that
guns were a bad idea. Not that I didn't teach my
children gun safety, because I did, but with Megan
Clark spending so much time with my children, and
given her ability to create chaos out of order, all the
gun-safety courses in the world wouldn't have
helped. I remember the time she and my daughter
Evin rewired our living room. Or rather Megan rewired it and Evin stood by and watched. I don't recall
why the girls did it, but we didn't have a working
light socket for weeks, until I hired Megan to put the
wiring back to rights. Can you imagine what she
could have done with a gun? It boggles my mind.
For one thing, she would have set out to arrest every
criminal in town. Megan has always had an overly
developed sense of fairness, which is a disadvantage
in today's social climate, and she has always disliked
criminals. I guess I shouldn't be surprised at her actions now. Nobody is more of a criminal than a murderer.

I unlocked my safe, whose combination Megan
was never able to figure out, mainly because I used
her birth date, which it never occurred to her to try,
and took out the Navy Colt I bought at an antique
gun show several years ago. It's one hundred and
twenty years old, and I hope it doesn't blow up in
my face. Also, I hope it still works. On the other
hand, it's big and deadly looking and reeks of history
and the Wild West and gunfights in dusty streets, and
ought to scare the bejesus out of any of our five suspects, so maybe I won't have to fire it at all.

When I picked up Megan, she was wearing her fruit-salad dress, which was actually a peach-colored frothy-looking concoction with what used to be called in my youth an Empire waist, but God only knows what it's called now. The dress ended on the high end of mid-thigh and in my opinion was too short, but who am I to know. Mostly, I hoped that Megan didn't fall off her shoes, which had to have five-inch heels at least. From hiking boots to five-inch heels is asking a lot of any woman, and with Megan's trick ankle—the result of a soccer injury she suffered when she stepped in a prairie-dog hole during a hard-fought game in the fourth grade—I figured I'd better stay close enough to catch her when she fell.

"My mother has no taste at all," Megan complained when she got in the car. "I feel like I'm dressed in peach Jell-O. I don't know why I couldn't wear my black cocktail dress."

"Is that the dress you wore when you were initiated into the National Honor Society your junior year in high school?"

"So?"

"And you wore it last year to the library Book and Author dinner?"

"So?"

"Megan, every seam above the waist in that dress dissolved during the main course, and I had to use Scotch tape to hold it together long enough to get you home without your being arrested for indecent exposure."

"I sewed up the seams."

I didn't comment. Megan barely knows which end of the needle to thread, and any sewing she does would not win a prize in 4-H. I think it's another heredity thing, since her mother was totally incompetent as a seamstress and used to curse like a sailor whenever she had to make a costume for one of Megan's many activities. My wife always made sure the windows were closed during one of these attempts, to try to cut down on our kids picking up any of the colorful vocabulary blaring out of the house next door.

"It's a beautiful dress, and you are a beautiful woman, so stop mourning your cocktail dress and enjoy looking good enough to eat."

She flipped down the visor and examined herself in the small mirror attached to it. "Do you really think I'm beautiful, or are you just being nice?"

"You're beautiful, so quit fidgeting and remember to keep your shoes on at least through the banquet."

"I brought my tennis shoes to wear when I'm meeting with our murderer so I can run if I need to," she said.

My stomach clenched and my chest felt as cold as if my heart and lungs had suddenly been frozen. i had a hard time drawing a breath. "Is that what the bulge in your purse is? Your tennis shoes? Where's your weapon? Your sockful of quarters, your brick, your gun!"

"I'll use my shoes as weapons if I need to, but I don't think I will."

"You know who it is, don't you?" I asked, glancing at her. She sat very still, but the sun hadn't set yet, and I saw a tear on her cheek. "Are you frightened, Megan? Is that why you're crying?"

She blotted her tears on the inner side of her hem, leaving a black smudge from her mascara. "No, I'm just mad. And maybe a little bit sad. I wish Clyde Brownleigh had never come to the convention, then he would be alive and Denise would be alive and no one would be killing his friends in order to get the manuscript. I wanted to put on a fun convention where all of us who loved string figures could get together and visit and maybe try to outdo each other on who could make the most complex figure. But hopes for that kind of a convention died when Clyde Brownleigh got up and made the announcement about the manuscript."

I turned into the parking lot of the High Plains Motel and parked near the door closest to the Sagebrush Room, where the banquet was to be held. I figured Megan might be able to totter into the banquet room in those five-inch heels if she didn't have to walk far. And I could take her arm to give her balance. Or catch her.

The banquet was held in the Palo Duro Room instead, as motel management and Dr. Moser agreed that the Sagebrush Room held bad memories for our group, an understatement if I ever heard one. All the ladies, who were mostly older than Megan, clustered around her to compliment her on the frothy peach concoction her mother had bought. Megan swayed on

her heels and acknowledged the compliments without
believing a one. She would accept being cute, but she
would never believe she was beautiful.

The men all hung around the edge of the crowd of
women and drooled. Sometimes I believe my fellowman, no matter how old, how educated, how cultured,
is lewd, crude, and generally disgusting under the
surface. Even Dr. Moser, who is probably beyond the
help of even Viagra, was looking at Megan with a
certain gleam in his eye. As for David Owen Lister,
if he licked his lips one more time, I intended to
empty the contents of the nearest pitcher of water
down the front of his trousers, where it would do the
most good. John Harper was nothing less than pa-
thetic, gazing at Megan as though she was an intricate
string figure he planned on unraveling at the first opportunity. Call Me Herb looked shell-shocked, which
was fine with me. It was better than the lustful eyes
of the other men. The only men who looked as if
they were unaffected by Megan's dress—which I still
thought was too low on one end and too high on the
other—were Dr. Yahara and the Reverend Wilson. I
presumed that religion was the cloak which protected
Wilson from his lustful nature, but I couldn't figure
out why Dr. Yahara remained oblivious to Megan's
charms, of which too much were on display, until I
happened to catch him looking at her, then dabbing
his forehead with his handkerchief. Apparently Megan brought out a feverish sweat in every man there.

Halfway through a fairly decent meal for a motel

banquet—edible chicken, a decent green salad made without iceberg lettuce, and green peas which had not been boiled—Megan excused herself and left the room. The gentlemen at the table—Lister, Dr. Moser, Dr. Yahara, John Harper, and the Reverend Wilson—assumed that she went to the ladies' room. Only Agnes and I—the only other people seated there who were in on the secret—knew the truth. Megan had tottered off in her five-inch heels to slip an invitation for a midnight meeting under the door of each gentleman's room. Agnes and I exchanged glances, as the condemned do, and I reached around under my coat to adjust my Navy Colt. I had tucked it in my belt in the middle of my back, and I was afraid it would slip through and fall on the floor. It being too big to hide in my coat pocket, my other choice was to tuck it inside my waistband, but I was afraid it would slip, and I might have to race to the men's room to retrieve a Navy Colt from my crotch. Worse, I was afraid the trigger would catch on my pants and shoot my behind off.

Her errand accomplished, Megan slipped back in her seat and clutched my hand under the table. Her face was composed, with lips just parted in a faint smile you might miss if you didn't look quickly, but her hand in mine was cold as ice. One might never know from looking that Megan Clark was about to challenge a killer for the sake of two people she didn't even like, but hold her hand, and you knew that she was scared.

She was the bravest woman I've ever known.

"So, Dr. Yahara, will you be returning to Japan immediately after the convention, or will you play tourist for a while?" asked Agnes in a cheery tone that sounded as if she wasn't about to hide in a coat closet to wait for a killer.

Frankly, I couldn't say a word without squeaking.

My God, but we were all insane.

"I plan to see your Palo Duro Canyon and spend a week at a ranch just outside town. That is, if the lieutenant lets us go," Yahara said.

"He doesn't have proof enough against any of you to hold you," said Megan, her voice sounding almost aggressive. Where do these women get their courage?

"Are you certain, Dr. Clark?" asked John Harper. "I need to get back to the Navajo reservation and collect some more string figures. I'm planning to write an article on seven different figures which are nearly identical to one another, but are from seven different Indian tribes. Basically, I'm discussing cross-culturalism."

Sounded fascinating—if you believed culturalism was a word.

"Dr. Moser, did you ever read Agatha Christie's *Ten Little Indians,* which is also known as *And Then There Were None*?" asked Megan.

"Actually, I don't read many mysteries, but I did see the movie, the version with Barry Fitzgerald and Walter Huston. I believe it was the first of the film versions in the United States—1945 seems to stick in my mind."

"I believe you're right," said Agnes. "I believe it

was 1945, and it's the best of the film versions in my opinion."

Megan wrinkled up her forehead, so I knew she had little patience for the interruptions. "I see a lot of comparisons between Christie's book and our little mystery. You all know the story: ten people invited for the weekend at a large home on an island. But the host is not there, and during the first evening, a recording by someone purporting to be him accuses each of the guests of a crime for which they were not punished. One by one the guests are murdered in ways that are similar to the verses of the old nursery rhyme 'Ten Little Indians.' "

"I'm a Christie fan and I don't see any resemblance at all," said the reverend.

"I haven't noticed any Indian figures on a mantelpiece," said Dr. Moser. "If we had a mantelpiece. If it *was* a mantelpiece in the movie, and I can't remember if it was or not."

"We don't have Indian figurines," said Megan, "but we have string figures. The first one is Cheating the Hangman—which of course, Clyde Brownleigh doesn't do, an irony in itself. There are dozens of figures which could have been used to strangle Brownleigh, but the murderer chooses this one. Why? Because he is punishing Brownleigh for a crime, a hanging offense. What did Brownleigh do? He committed blasphemy. He attempted to sell for money a sacred text, and to string-figure enthusiasts, anything by Caroline Furness Jayne is a sacred text. I heard someone call *String Figures and How to Make Them* the bible of string-figure enthusiasts. And according to Brownleigh, this manuscript contained the directions for making the Nauru Island figures and several Inuit string figures. Imagine how the Christian world would react if there was only one copy of the Holy Bible, and a man like Brownleigh tried to sell it to the highest bidder. That is how string-figure enthusiasts feel about the Jayne manuscript."

All at the table were silent, eyes fixed on Megan, but this time there were no expressions of lust in the men's eyes. There was, however, puzzlement and apprehension. I was a little puzzled myself. As for apprehension, I was way past that point and closing in on panic.

Megan continued, her face was still composed, but her expression was growing more and more stern. "Then the second murder, that of Denise LeClerc, a miserable young woman who seemed to dislike everyone, including herself. What was her crime other than self-hatred? I think it was blackmail. She saw me leaving Brownleigh's room, but she also saw someone else—one of you."

"Excuse me," said David Lister. "I don't have to sit here and listen to this garbage. What is it with you, anyway? What's all this business about Agatha Christie and how Brownleigh and LeClerc's murders are like some in a book?"

"Obviously you're not a mystery fan," said John Harper. "I am, but mostly of the classic writers—Christie, Sayers, Chandler, G. K. Chesterton. But I don't follow you, Dr. Clark. What are you saying?

That the string figures we've made this weekend are clues?"

"Cheating the Hangman was," said Megan. "But Denise's murder was in a sense done by her own hand. If she had chosen not to drink that last cup of coffee, she would still be alive. Or maybe not. Blackmailers usually end up dead. The string figure she was making when she died is fitting, however. The Moon Goes Dark. The moon is a woman who goes dark—or dies. It is the moon in eclipse. However, that she was constructing that particular figure I believe is coincidence, but it is a coincidence that adds to the terror most of us felt. But Denise died because she was blackmailing the murderer, and what do you think she wanted in exchange for her silence? Money? I doubt it. I think she wanted the manuscript. Again, someone wanted to defile Jayne's work."

"I still don't see how this is similar to *Ten Little Indians*," said the reverend.

"Think about it. Why did the ten people on the island die? Because they were judged and sentence passed. The mysterious host was executing the sentences. Like those ten people, we have been metaphorically locked away for a weekend. Like Agatha Christie's characters, we have been judged by—someone, and some of us were found lacking. Brownleigh and LeClerc were judged, sentence passed, execution completed."

"Hey, lady," said David Lister, "I don't care about any of this mystery crap. What burns me is the way you come out and say that one of us is guilty. Where do you get off saying that?"

"All of you bid on the manuscript, and only those who bid on the manuscript went into Brownleigh's room, and it's a little difficult to strangle a man without going into his room to get close to him."

"So what do you think, that we got somebody playing judge here?" asked David Lister.

"That's exactly what I think," said Megan.

"Then string figures are not clues," said Reverend Wilson, staring into his coffee, then dipping the end of his left little finger to taste. I didn't blame him. I passed up coffee myself, and opted for a canned soft drink, which I nonetheless examined closely for holes.

"Cheating the Hangman is," argued Megan. "Judge, jury, executioner. The murderer is saying that the guilty won't get away again."

"I didn't kill Brownleigh and I didn't kill LeClerc, although I don't know how she lived as long as she did, considering how mean she was," said David Lister. "Besides, I was manning my booth and wasn't even in the Sagebrush Room for more than a minute or two."

"That was all it took," said Megan. "The poison was in the coffee cream."

David Lister and Reverend Wilson dropped the containers of cream they had just picked up.

19

*There is one infallible method of determining hu-
man guilt and responsibility... The truth can be
learned only by an analysis of the psychological fac-
tors of a crime, and the application of them to the
individual. The only real clues are psychological—
not material.*

—S. S. Van Dine,
in *The Benson Murder Case*, 1926

Megan kept taking deep breaths, and knew she
was in danger of hyperventilating. She must
calm down so she could think rationally. She was
surrounded by members of Murder by the Yard, and
the moment she was in danger, they would all come
to her rescue. Not that she thought she would need
to be rescued. Obviously, no one appreciated the
damage that a pair of shoes with five-inch heels could
do if used as a weapon. Grab one of those suckers
by the toes and use it as you would a hammer, and
Katie bar the door, because somebody was going to
have some good-sized holes in their anatomy.

She paced about the room, passing Ryan crouched
in a corner behind an upholstered chair. He was holding his Navy Colt, resting it on one knee. He was so
sweet, always worried about her and the first to de-

fend her. She just hoped he didn't shoot his foot off.

There was a soft knock on the door and she consulted her schedule. This should be John Harper, and he was right on time. She tapped on the coat closet door to alert Agnes as she walked by. She opened the door and stepped back. "Come in, John, and let's see if we can do any business."

John Harper looked stricken, as though all his illusions were shattered. "You're a hypocrite, Dr. Clark. All that talk at dinner and all the time you had the manuscript. Did you strangle Clyde Brownleigh, too?"

Harper's face was flushed, and he clenched and unclenched his fists. Megan knew he wanted to hit something or someone, preferably her, but like Ryan, he was too much of a gentleman to do it.

"Of course not. And I didn't kill Denise either. I merely stole the manuscript after someone else killed Brownleigh. Denise saw me leaving Brownleigh's room at one o'clock, although I've told everyone that I was in his room at twelve-thirty. I had to lie, because otherwise you would know I saw you."

Harper looked bewildered. In fact, he looked so bewildered that Megan was convinced he was innocent. Not that she took much convincing. In her opinion, John Harper couldn't kill a cockroach without going into mourning.

"I wasn't in Brownleigh's room at one o'clock or any other time except at ten-thirty when I had an appointment, and I didn't see you except at the bar, and you were giggling. I didn't come here to be accused of murder. All I want is the manuscript. It needs to be examined, and who better than a graduate student in anthropology? Of course, you're a Ph.D., but you're not worthy. I can give you a promissory note on some property I own near Santa Fe in exchange for the manuscript. Do we have a deal or not?"

Harper took a piece of paper out of his pocket, and it really was a promissory note. Once he overcame his shock that the author of the anonymous invitation was Megan, he got right down to business.

Megan sank onto the couch. "Forget it, John. I don't have the manuscript and you didn't murder Clyde Brownleigh."

Harper looked even more bewildered than he had before, if that was possible. "I don't understand."

"It was a trap, John. I'm hoping to uncover the murderer by offering to sell the manuscript."

"But you don't have the manuscript?"

Megan knew that a literal mind had some advantages in the academic world, but John Harper carried it too far. "No, I don't."

"Who does?" he asked, and Megan wondered just how bright John Harper really was. Obviously, the murderer stole the manuscript. Therefore, the murderer had the manuscript, or at least he did for a time.

"No one," said Megan. "No one has the manuscript."

"I don't understand," said Harper.

"Don't worry about it, John. I could still be wrong."

Harper walked around the hospitality room in an aimless manner. "This hasn't been a fun convention at all."

His voice had a whine in it that Megan thought most unattractive "I didn't expect two murders, John. I don't think you can hold me responsible for them. I certainly would have done my best to have prevented them if I had known," she said.

"I suppose you're not to blame. It's just that I wanted the manuscript, and I don't know who I'll have to argue with now that Denise is gone. She was an awful pain, but she did keep things stirred up and people on their toes."

Megan hoped he wouldn't start crying before she got him out of the room. On the other hand, she was very glad that Denise had at least one mourner. Everyone should have at least one person who would cry at their funeral.

She opened the door. "Go to bed, John. The convention is over."

He wandered through the door and stood scratching his head for a moment. "Are you sure you don't have the manuscript?"

"Cross my heart, hope to die." She could sense Ryan wince at the latter phrase. "Now go to bed, John. It's been a long weekend. And I would appreciate it if you didn't tell any of the others that it's me that left the invitations if you should meet anybody in the hall."

"I'll keep your secret because I'm embarrassed to

have anybody know I'm so greedy as to meet with a murderer for the manuscript."

"I'm not a murderer," Megan pointed out.

"I guess not, but I wouldn't want to be in your shoes if the real murderer came calling."

He wandered down the hall toward his room, still scratching his head, and Megan sighed. "That was a washout," she said to the hidden members of Murder by the Yard.

Agnes peeked out of the hall closet. "I always thought he was too nice a boy to be strangling people, Megan, but I suppose you had to be sure."

"Yes, I do," she said. "I want to be absolutely sure."

There was another knock at the door, and Megan took several deep breaths. This should be David Owen Lister, and she didn't much like him under the best of circumstances, much less putting up with his fit when he found out she had summoned him under false pretenses.

She opened the door. "Come in, David."

He walked in and looked her up and down in such a fashion that Megan felt she had been stripped to her underwear. "Well, if it isn't Ms. Ph.D. So you offed Brownleigh and stole the manuscript. Now you want to sell it to the highest bidder. That ain't me, Ms. Dr. Clark. I've got a little money, but not much. My aim was not to buy the manuscript, but to pay to set it in type so I could print several hundred copies to meet the demand of all the string-figure enthusiasts. I didn't want to keep it. Hell, the reverend could have it for his cultural center for all I care. I just wanted to make sure that if anybody wanted a copy, they could buy one. Not everybody could afford to go to a museum or archive."

"I misjudged you," said Megan. "And I'm sorry."

"You sure misjudged me if you thought I had much money."

"I don't have the manuscript," said Megan.

"Somebody buy it already?" David asked. "Tell me who and I'll approach them about printing the manuscript."

"It's a trap, David. I am trying to catch a killer. I don't have the manuscript, but I wanted to see who showed up wanting to buy it. If I'm correct, the killer will show up and try to add me to his repertoire of victims."

David stood rubbing his chin and looking at her. "You got guts, lady, but not many brains. Let the cops catch the killer. It's what we pay them for."

"You sound like Ryan," said Megan.

"I'd listen to him. You'll live longer." He opened the door and wandered out.

"David!" Megan called in a loud whisper. "Please don't tell any of the others."

"Are you kidding? You might not think much of me, but I don't want a murder on my conscience." With that, he turned and walked away.

"Even David Lister gives good advice occasionally," said Ryan from behind the chair.

"Don't let him scare you, Megan. We won't let

anyone hurt you," said Candi in a muffled voice from under the couch.

Megan let a giggle escape. Anyone who happened to walk in would think the furniture was talking.

"It's not funny, Megan!" said Ryan in a loud whisper.

There was a soft knock on the door, and Megan opened it. "Dr. Moser, come in."

The old man walked slowly to the couch, leaning on his cane with every step. "I take it this is a trap, Miss Megan?"

"Do you want to deal?" asked Megan, swallowing the bile that threatened to choke her. "I'm accepting bids on the manuscript."

"Oh, my dear, I'm entirely too old to play games. I leave that to younger and more foolish men, speaking of which, I imagine your Dr. Stevens is lurking about somewhere."

"I'm behind the chair, Dr. Moser," came Ryan's muffled voice.

"I thought as much. That interesting invitation that someone slid under my door was obviously a phony. Miss Megan, the handwriting was indisputably that of a woman, and you were the only woman who left the banquet for any extended length of time."

"I never thought about my handwriting," said Megan. "But no one else said anything."

"Dr. Yahara and I are the only teachers among the bidders, and the language barrier might prevent Tomoyuki from distinguishing gender in English handwriting, but not me. I spent entirely too many years deciphering students' handwriting." He paused and rested both hands on his cane. "But tell me, Miss Megan, what is this nonsense of a game you're playing, you and I imagine your mystery-reading friends?"

"I am hoping to uncover the murderer," said Megan, biting her lower lip. There was no one like an elderly person to make her feel foolish, and Dr. Moser was very elderly.

"A foolish goal, my dear Miss Megan. If I figured out this—what should I call it?—scam, then the others can, too."

"They haven't so far," said Megan, sounding on the defensive even to her own ears.

"Who has come so far?" asked Dr. Moser.

"David Lister and John Harper—and you."

"I hardly came for the same purpose that they did. Such greedy young men, although I wouldn't have thought it of John Harper. He seems too—earnest. I've always found the earnest to also be honest."

"I thought David Lister was just greedy, too, but I've changed my mind," said Megan, feeling an urgency to defend the cyberspace merchant. "He really wants to publish the manuscript so every string-figure enthusiast can afford a copy. You know how difficult it is to persuade a museum or archive to publish. If the manuscript ended up in Reverend Wilson's cultural center or Denise's museum, I doubt it would ever be published. Even John Harper was planning to use it in his dissertation, and not many dissertations are published."

"I doubt one on string figures would be published. The subject is not exactly of worldwide interest."

"Maybe not, but I stand by what I said. I misjudged the two men, especially David Lister. There is a core of altruism in him that no one would expect."

"He'll make money off Caroline Furness Jayne," insisted the old man.

"I don't think so, not enough to make it worthwhile anyway. The profit margin on most books is very low, Dr. Moser. David would have to sell thousands of copies to make even a marginal profit. Ask Agnes."

Dr. Moser grinned. "And I suppose that Agnes is lurking behind the potted plant in the corner?"

"No, that's Lorene. Agnes is in the coat closet, Rosemary's in the pantry, Herb's upstairs, Candi's under the couch, and Randal is lurking in the bush outside the sliding-glass door."

The old man laughed until tears came to his eyes. "Oh, Miss Megan, if only I had met you when I was thirty, or even sixty—I was a very frisky sixty—I might have tried to sweep you off your feet. But I didn't, and I wouldn't want to live my life over. I probably wouldn't do any better the second time through. But, my dear, I beg of you, please don't continue this dangerous game. Even your friends can't save you from a bullet through the heart as you walk down the hall or across the parking lot."

"The hell you say!"exclaimed Ryan as he leaped from behind the chair, his Navy Colt cocked and ready.

"Bravo!" Dr. Moser applauded. "Wonderful! An Old West figure ready to protect his woman. However, I would suggest you use that old Colt to bludgeon the bad guy rather than risk firing it."

"I'll do what I have to do," said Ryan, and Megan felt tears burning her eyes. Ryan was such a sweetie.

Dr. Moser hauled himself up with the aid of Megan and his cane. "If I can't persuade you that this is not a good idea, then I'll go on back to my room and keep my fingers crossed."

"You haven't asked me about the manuscript, Dr. Moser," said Megan as the old man maneuvered his way to the door.

"Why should I, my dear? You don't have the manuscript."

"How do you know?"

"The murderer has the manuscript, Miss Megan, and you are not a murderer." He tapped on the door of the coat closet. "Hello, Agnes, I hope you're staying cool in there. I thought the motel was a little too warm today."

"The murderer does not have the manuscript," Megan said to Dr. Moser's back.

The old man turned around, his eyes narrowed. "Then who has it, pray tell?"

"No one," she answered.

"Smart girl," he said. "I agree."

"What are you two talking about?" asked Ryan,

his eyes darting around the room as if there might be outlaws instead of Murder by the Yard members hiding there.

"Never mind, Ryan. I'll explain later," said Megan. "Good night, Dr. Moser, and please keep my secret."

"No, it won't be a good night. Few of them are anymore. But I will let you play out your game without interference."

"Is that a promise?" Megan asked.

Dr. Moser paused in the doorway for several seconds. "If I can't persuade you that your efforts are futile, then I promise."

"I know most of the story, Dr. Moser, so I doubt that in the end my efforts will be futile," she called after the old man as he shuffled down the hall.

"You ought to listen to Dr. Moser and give this nonsense up, Megan," said Ryan. "Honey, I can't protect you against a bullet."

Megan whirled around to look at him. He'd used that endearment again, and she still wasn't sure what he meant by it. She wasn't even sure what her reaction should be.

"There won't be a bullet. I guarantee it," she said.

"Just how the devil do you know that?" demanded Ryan, his legs spread apart in a gunfighter's stance and his Colt held at waist height.

"Because all our suspects flew into Amarillo, and it's very difficult to get a gun through airport security, and they haven't left the motel, so unless they bought a Saturday-night special from one of the motel employees, they are unarmed. Besides, none of them anticipated Clyde Brownleigh, so they didn't come prepared for a shoot-out. I think I'm safe enough from a bullet through the heart or head." Megan swallowed hard to try to force the lump in her throat back to wherever it had come from.

"You'd trust your life on that reasoning?" asked Ryan.

"I don't have a choice."

20

MAN CLIMBING A TREE

A figure from Australia.

1. Opening A.

2. Turn the hands so the palms face you and 5 (Right and Left Little Fingers) goes over all the Loops and picks up 4n (near string on Right and Left Ring Finger) and returns.

3. Navajo the 5 Loops (lift the Lower Loop with your teeth over the Right and Left Little Finger Loops).

4. There is a Palmar String that crosses the 2 Loop (Loop on Right and Left Index Fingers) on each hand. Hook the 2 (Right and Left Index Fingers) fingers down over the Palmar Strings and hold them down to the palms.

5. Put your foot in the large Loop held by the 5 (Right and Left Little Fingers) fingers.

6. Drop the 1 Loops (Loops on Right and Left Thumbs) and pull gently with your 2 (Right and Left Index Fingers) fingers.

7. To make the man climb the tree, alternate gently pulling the right and left fingers.

Dr. Moser's mention of guns scared the bejesus out of me. I don't even like to contemplate Megan being hurt, much less killed. To be honest, I don't know if I could survive her death. I loved my wife and would have happily lived out my life with her had she not died, but my attachment to Megan is in some ways stronger. She is my spirit, my soul, that bright spot that fills my life with light. Our relationship is different from the one I had with my wife, and Megan will never replace her, but then she will never need to. She has her own place in my life, and if she is not in love with me, it doesn't matter. I love her and that is enough. There, I admitted it. I love her—which explains why I turn pea green whenever Jerry Carr shows up. Thank God he is too much of a klutz and an idiot to appreciate that she is a very astute detective, because he will never further his cause with her if he doesn't recognize her unique intellect.

But at that moment I wished we had Jerry Carr here with all his henchmen and henchwomen, because the cold spot in my chest just kept growing. There was something going on that I couldn't fathom, and it frightened me.

There was another knock on the door and I dived behind the chair and scooted back until I was in the corner and unable to be seen unless someone climbed up in the chair and looked over the back.

"Come in, Dr. Yahara," I heard Megan say, and I

gripped my Navy Colt tighter. What if Yahara is the
murderer and he uses some Oriental unarmed combat
trick on her? I thought. Of course, it had better work
the first time, or Megan would kick the devil out of
him. After thirteen years of dance and some eight
years of crew—that's the word for the rowing
teams—Megan's legs are strong enough to kick
down a solid-core door, and if she follows it up with
an attack armed with her five-inch heels, then Yahara
will be lucky to survive until the paramedics arrive.
But that's if he's not a kung fu master, or is kung fu
Chinese unarmed combat? I'm not very knowledgeable in the field beyond what I learned watching
Chuck Norris movies.

"Dr. Megan Clark, you are the one who has the
manuscript?" Dr. Yahara asked.

"Why do you sound so surprised, Dr. Yahara?"
asked Megan with that aggressive tone she'd used
with everyone but Dr. Moser.

"Because I expected you to have more honor."

Ouch! That hurt. I could feel Megan cringe all the
way behind the chair.

"This is about money, not honor. Are you prepared
to make an offer, Dr. Yahara?"

"I have power of attorney to sign over my family's
import business," said the Japanese professor.

"Why are you willing to spend your family into
poverty just to have the Jayne manuscript?" asked
Megan.

"Because she was a woman who saw beauty in a
folk art dismissed by most of the civilized world as

'children's games.' To be able to see beauty and bring it forth to the world that it might not be lost is an achievement that sets apart this woman from others. Unlike yourself, she was an honorable woman."

Ouch again! That may have hurt more than Dr. Yahara's last insult. Without seeing Megan, I knew her face was turning pale. The blood always flushes out of her face when she faces danger or insults.

I heard the crackle of paper, which meant Megan was studying the deed to see if it was genuine or not. "What do you plan to do with the manuscript, Dr. Yahara?" I heard her ask.

"I will publish it so others might enjoy the string figures, but the manuscript itself I will keep safe in my home in a glass case, and when I die, I will leave it to the University of Pennsylvania, where so many of her family taught."

"Here is your deed, Dr. Yahara. I don't have the manuscript."

"Then the note, it was not from you?" he asked, and I could hear the puzzlement in his voice. If she had accomplished nothing else, Megan Clark had succeeded in fooling a lot of people that night.

"It was from me, but I don't have the manuscript."

"I did not sense violence in you, but I knew if you had the manuscript, then you were the killer of Brownleigh and LeClerc. But you say you do not have the manuscript, so you did not strangle Brownleigh?" asked Yahara.

"I've never murdered anyone, but I'm angry that there was murder at my convention. I didn't like

Brownleigh and Denise LeClerc, but I don't condone their murders, and want the person responsible to pay the consequences," Megan said in that stern voice of hers.

She seldom sounds stern because her natural voice is, well, sweet. And I'm not prejudiced. She has a sweet voice. So if she sounds stern, you can count on Megan Clark doing whatever is necessary to set things right. Unfortunately, setting things right the last few months had involved murders, specifically, those who commit them.

"It is an honorable goal, and many apologies for doubting your honor, but I could think nothing else."

"Apologies accepted. Tell me, Dr. Yahara, who do you think murdered Clyde Brownleigh and Denise LeClerc?"

The silence drew itself out until I was ready to leap out from behind my chair. Finally, he answered. "I will not think closely on that question."

"Does that mean you don't want to know?"

"Exactly. These men, these 'usual suspects,' as your lieutenant calls us, are comrades of mine. I have known some of them many years, others not so long. I did not know Clyde Brownleigh at all. I do not wish to know which one of my comrades is guilty."

"But what about Denise? Didn't you know her for many years? Don't you feel angry that someone killed her?" There was a sound of urgency in Megan's voice that I didn't understand.

"Dr. LeClerc was, as you called her, a wicked woman who lived to cause chaos. She invited murder each day of her life, and murder finally accepted her invitation. I cannot grieve that she achieved what she had been seeking: death. It is unfortunate that she died without honor, but she had not honor while she lived, so how can one expect it at her death," said Dr. Yahara.

"I can't accept that theory," said Megan, beginning to pace.

"The young are so much more unforgiving than the old," said Dr. Yahara. "I will return to my room now, and I give you this advice: don't disturb what has been done here."

"So you're warning me how dangerous it is to challenge a murderer," said Megan.

"It may be, it may not be, but this I know: it is better left alone."

I heard the door shut quietly, and rose out of my crouch. "He's a strange duck, but even he warned you against messing around with killers."

Megan shook her head. "No, he didn't. He warned me about disturbing the status quo. That's not the same thing."

"It's close enough for government work, Megan. Let's drop it and go home. I want to put this gun back in the safe before it accidently goes off and emasculates me."

"I wouldn't be shoving it in my waistband in that case. You don't want to spend the rest of your life with a squeaky voice," said Megan.

I pulled my gun out of my waistband.

The last knock of the night came, a solid sound with some fist in it. I crouched down again, with my Colt at the ready. I vowed I'd take the Colt to a gun shop first thing Monday morning and have it put in working order. With Megan, I never knew when I might be playing a white knight.

"Reverend Wilson, come in," said Megan.

"I never expected you after our conversations at dinner tonight. I am very disappointed that you have committed such crimes, and that now you want to profit from your deeds. I want the manuscript very badly, but I will not reward you for raising your hand against your fellowman."

If you want to hear disapproving, you ought to hear Reverend Robert Wilson. I was ready to confess my sins, and I couldn't remember committing any lately. Unless you consider the lust in my heart for Megan in her peach-colored confection. I'd be back to normal tomorrow when she was wearing her hiking boots and carpenter pants.

"It's good that you don't want to pay me for the manuscript, Reverend, because I don't have it."

"I beg your pardon?"

"I don't have the manuscript."

"But why did you slip a note under my door offering to sell it?" The good reverend sounded puzzled, too.

"To see who would come to my party. The person who didn't come would know it was a trap because he is the one who sent Brownleigh and LeClerc to their premature rewards. Sorry, Reverend, I just couldn't resist the religious lingo."

"It's quite all right, because I can't resist it either. It's in the blood, you know. But, young woman, speaking of blood, you might find some of yours spilled if you persist in this challenge to a murderer. I know a bit more about murderers than you do, because I was once a prison chaplain. A real murderer, as opposed to someone who snapped under stress and killed without really meaning to—a real murderer doesn't think like you or I. They see no reason not to kill if that's the best way to get what they might want."

"Who do you think murdered Brownleigh and LeClerc?" asked Megan.

"I don't know, and I try not to spend any time speculating about it. I really don't want to think ill of my fellowman—that's why I was a very bad prison chaplain—and I particularly don't want to think ill of my fellowman if I know him well, and I knew all of those at the table tonight very well."

"Thank you, Reverend. I hope your mission work in the Northern Territories goes well."

I heard a door close and finally stood up and put my gun in my pocket. The grip was visible, and there is no way that anyone would mistake it for anything but a gun, but it was late enough now that all the guests should be in bed. With any luck I could make it home without either shooting off some vital part of myself or shooting someone else.

"All right, everybody out. The evening is over and

the trap didn't work. If you've been listening, then you know we stayed up late to spring a trap that never sprang," said Megan.

Agnes stepped out of the closet and sneezed six times in a row. "Thank goodness I was able to hold them in until the last man was out the door. I don't think I've ever been in a closet that is so dusty!"

"And I'm going to have to go to the chiropractor early Monday morning," said Lorene. "Crouching behind that potted plant has given me a stiff back."

Rosemary stepped out of the pantry. "It's a good thing I'm not claustrophobic. That pantry is no bigger than a coffin. Someone had better check on Candi. Apparently she's still under the couch."

Call Me Herb and I lifted the couch off a sleeping Candi. It's good that she doesn't snore, or Megan wouldn't have had an opportunity to run her sting on the usual suspects, all of whom seem to be innocent, by the way. If it weren't for two bodies very definitely dead by illegal means, I would wonder that murder was committed at all.

Megan woke up Candi and sent her to get Randal out of the bush, then flopped down on the couch. "I'm sorry I kept you all up so late. My trap didn't work quite the way I thought it would, but thank you for helping me. I felt safe with all of you here."

I don't know why she should have. Her defense consisted of three elderly woman, three men in their forties, one of whom is an anal-retentive lawyer, a young woman with an ill-fitting pair of contacts, a pair of shoes with five-inch heels, and a Navy Colt which probably hasn't been fired in a hundred years.

As I said before, I think we are insane.

"I guess I'll see you on Thursday at Time and Again, and we'll finally discuss *'A' Is for Alibi* by Sue Grafton," said Megan.

"I think our next book ought to be one of the Henry O series by Caroline Hart," said Rosemary, nudging her friend to get her attention. "Henry O is our age, Lorene, or nearly so. She not only solves murders, she has a sex life."

"Let's discuss it at the bookstore on Thursday," said Megan. "I'm too tired to think about it now."

I ushered the others out and turned to Megan, who was putting on her five-inch heels.

"Why don't you leave your tennis shoes on, Megan, we're going right home."

"I want to go see Dr. Moser, Ryan. I need to ask him a question. Go on out to the truck, and I'll be out in about fifteen minutes."

"I'll go with you."

She shook her head. "I don't think he will talk as freely in front of you, Ryan, and I need some information from him to solve these murders."

"I thought you told Murder by the Yard that the trap remained unsprung."

"Please, Ryan, I'm too tired to argue."

I should have been suspicious then. Megan is never too tired to argue. Megan is too young to recognize tired as anything but an abstract concept.

"All right, I'll wait for you." It was a grudging agreement, but I made it.

I went out to my truck and slipped in a cassette of what is called easy-listening music. I leaned my head back and closed my eyes. When I woke up, Megan had been gone a lot longer than any fifteen minutes, and my gun had disappeared from my pocket. I was out of my truck and running for Dr. Moser's room, but I was too late.

21

"Come in."

Megan opened Dr. Moser's door and walked in, feeling the weight of Ryan's Navy Colt in her purse. "Good evening again, Dr. Moser."

"You're a very brave woman, Miss Megan. It's dangerous to pretend to be a murderer and a thief in the presence of the real McCoy."

Dr. Moser sat in the room's easy chair with his feet on the matching hassock, and Megan couldn't see a weapon anywhere on him. Of course, that's not to say that he didn't have a syringe of nicotine poison ready to jab in her arm at a moment's notice.

"You don't have the character to murder for gain, so I'm guessing that you murdered Brownleigh to prevent him from selling Caroline Jayne's manuscript for profit," said Megan, easing down into a straight-back chair in front of the room's dresser.

"In a manner of speaking. I killed Brownleigh because he dared to use a saintly woman's reputation to turn a dollar," said Dr. Moser. "That is unspeakable."

"When did you realize the manuscript was a forgery?" asked Megan.

"How do you know it was? You never examined it," retorted Dr. Moser.

"Lorene and Rosemary described the pages they saw as thick and yellowing. That's when I knew it was a fake. Caroline Furness Jayne would have used the best paper, which in those days was rag paper. Rag paper doesn't yellow nearly as quickly as our modern wood-pulp paper. I have books on my shelves at home that are nearly three hundred years old, and the paper is nearly as white as the day the book was printed."

"Very good, but then you're an archaeologist by trade, are you not?"

"And a physical anthropologist. Actually, I'm a paleopathologist."

Dr. Moser sighed. "That's why you could learn so much from the two victims. I never expected that, because I accepted you too much at face value—sweet, cute, and nice. I should have added smart to that list. But to return to the manuscript, yes, it was a fake. Had it not been, I simply would have outbid everyone—I'm quite wealthy, you know—and saved Caroline Furness Jayne's work from the crude uses to which the others would have put it."

"In a way I helped you commit the murder," said Megan. "I kicked him, which I imagine slowed him down a little."

"He was walking all hunched over, but I didn't need your help. I offered to show Brownleigh how to construct Cheating the Hangman. I stood behind him while he sat in a chair, and when the loop was around his neck, I suddenly pulled it as taut as I could. If Brownleigh had been the least bit intelligent, he would have used his greater strength against me, but instead he panicked, pulling at the string. I've made string figures all my life, so my fingers and hands are quick and supple and very strong, much stronger that the rest of my body. I cut off his oxygen with the first yank, and then it was a matter of hanging on and keeping the string taut."

Dr. Moser paused to sip out his drink—vodka, judging by the bottle by his arm. "But tell me, Miss Megan, how did you know I was the guilty one."

"There were several things, one being the fact that the manuscript had not been found. If it had been in the motel, Jerry Carr would have found it. That meant to me that the manuscript no longer existed, and if it didn't, then it was a fake, which you would recognize. Another fact is your obsession with Caroline Furness Jayne. Obsession would be required to strangle a man, I would think. Also, you had the best opportunity to poison Denise's cream because you were sitting by her at the podium, and you were the one who asked me to order another urn of coffee. And like most women, Denise sat her purse down by her chair, which made it easy for you to pick her pocket. You took the syringe from her emergency glucose kit, filled it with nicotine poison, and injected it into the cream. I am assuming, of course, that you knew Denise was diabetic, since you had known her for several years."

Dr. Moser nodded. "It's difficult for a diabetic to hide her condition from an astute observer, and I had, as you said, known her for a long time. But go on, Miss Megan, tell me what else gave me away."

"The missing cream container. I wouldn't have had a clue as to what you did with it had Randal Anderson not pointed out what any teacher would know: kids stick contraband underneath their desks with chewing gum. You stuck the container underneath your chair while Special Crimes searched you, then you had to 'rest' in that same chair for a while before leaving the Sagebrush Room. You took the opportunity to remove the container from underneath your chair and left the room. I imagine you burned the container, since, as you pointed out, you smoke cigars."

"I am most impressed by you, Miss Megan. If Lieutenant Carr had the intelligence of a gnat, he would hire you on as a consultant." Dr. Moser paused to take another swallow of his vodka. "Do go on and tell me more."

"The metal cup in which you prepared the nicotine poison was tossed on top of the other trash in the Dumpster, where it could be easily seen. Now, wouldn't the murderer push that cup down into the Dumpster so Special Crimes would have had to look for it? But if the murderer is ninety-six years old, he might lack the strength to grub around in the trash. Oh, and another thing, the details of Brownleigh's murder are not quite the way you described it. The murderer used some object to gain leverage in order to twist Cheating the Hangman so tightly around Brownleigh's neck that the cord was buried in his flesh. I thought at first of a pencil or a ballpoint pen, but I was wrong, wasn't I? You used your cane."

Dr. Moser nodded. "Canes are useful for more than one purpose."

"I don't quite know how you learned about Denise."

"Very simple and quite by accident. I stepped outside the Sagebrush Room to visit with Dr. Stevens for a moment. He was listening so intently to Denise's interrogation that he fell out of his chair. He really didn't have to put out so much effort, since Denise has always had the loudest speaking voice of anyone I know. I heard her mention seeing you coming out of Brownleigh's room at one o'clock. I knew that was wrong because I was in his room around one. Denise saw me, not you, but being Denise, she wanted to cause as much trouble as possible. Later, of course, she demanded the manuscript in front of you and the others."

"But she demanded the manuscript of everyone," Megan protested.

"Denise was a professor of English, Megan, When she spoke of my possible plans for the manuscript, she used the present tense. She knew I took that manuscript. Had she been a wiser woman, she would have known better than to taunt a man who had just strangled his first victim. But she wasn't—and she wasn't a likable, admirable woman either, but most of all, she also planned to subvert the work of a beautiful, gracious, loving woman in the name of her cause. Caroline Furness Jayne was and is appreciated by anthropologists everywhere. She doesn't need the help of a narrow-minded shrew. So I killed Denise, and I can't say that I regret it. I brewed nicotine by boiling my Havana cigars according to a recipe that I got off the Internet. It recommended five drops in her cream. I used six."

He sat back, picked up his glass of vodka, and drained it. "I used six in my drink, too. I don't care to embarrass my family over this affair."

"Dr. Moser, no!" screamed Megan.

"Oh, yes, my dear. Ninety-six is a very great age and I'm very tired."

Megan heard the convulsions start as she got an outside line to dial 911.

EPILOGUE

Librarians are wonderful people. They should be in the detective business.

—WILSON TUCKER,
in *The Chinese Doll*, 1946

I drove to the bookstore for the first meeting after Dr. Moser's suicide because I didn't trust Megan to drive. It had only been four days since the end of the ill-fated convention, the day Megan watched Dr. Moser die, and she was still shaky. Not that she actually physically shook, but her complexion had a waxy appearance, and she looked older, even though I couldn't see any lines or wrinkles on her face. She had not yet come to terms with what she had seen, and it was making her sick in ways few understood. Megan might be a palepathologist and used to working with the dead, but there is a difference between that and what she experienced this weekend. Megan watched Dr. Moser cross that border between the quick and the dead by his own choice, and I don't believe she had ever witnessed that before. I never have and I'm older than she. Oh, we both saw Denise die a violent death, but it was like Dr. Yahara said: Denise invited her own murder, which made it less horrible than it should have been. You might think less of me for agreeing with Dr. Yahara, but his words were true. But, however you categorize the corpses, Megan Clark has been involved in three deaths over a single weekend. No wonder she looked a little pasty.

I thought Murder by the Yard Reading Circle ought to postpone until next week—or next month. I even suggested disbanding, but Megan gave me one of those looks—where she narrows her eyes and pins your carcass to the nearest wall if a barn door isn't handy—and snapped off a few words in a tone cold enough to delay a spring thaw until summer.

"Don't be ridiculous, Ryan!"

I didn't want to invite any more sharp words, so I shut up and drove the rest of the way in silence.

All the members were present, and all barely let Megan get herself a cup of coffee before the questions flew.

"When did you first suspect Dr. Moser?"

"How did you know the manuscript was a fake?"

"When did he inject the poison into the coffee cream?"

"Weren't you terrified to face him by yourself?" asked Lorene.

"No," said Megan. "I thought I was safe because I was—respectful."

"What does that mean exactly?" asked Randal, crossing one leg over the other and folding his arms. It was his combative pose, so I figured he was set to argue with Megan the rest of the evening. I hoped he would. A good argument would improve Megan's spirits.

"I didn't plan to turn a buck with that manuscript. I thought Caroline Furness Jayne too wonderful a woman to exploit her work. Dr. Moser knew that. Not that he would have killed anyone else. I don't think he would."

I thought Agnes looked a little dubious about the good doctor's harmlessness after he disposed of Brownleigh and Denise, but she said nothing. Not until the meeting was over and Megan and I were the last ones to leave did Agnes finally ask the question no one else thought of.

"If Dr. Moser was so wealthy, why didn't he just outbid everyone else for the manuscript? Then it would have been his to destroy. Why did he have to kill Brownleigh? And why not tell Denise that the manuscript was a forgery and that he had destroyed it? Then it wouldn't be necessary to kill Denise."

Megan smiled. "Dr. Moser would be so proud of you for thinking of those questions. But he told me his motives. Brownleigh was unspeakable. He besmirched an icon. In Dr. Moser's opinion, he had to die. And Denise. Do you think Denise would have believed Dr. Moser if he told her he destroyed the manuscript? But even if she did, she still saw him leave Brownleigh's room. She *knew* he was the murderer. Would you trust Denise to keep a secret like that? Denise, who deliberately put pages of the forged manuscript in Candi's purse just because she was angry?" Megan shook her head. "No, Denise had to die."

Agnes looked pensive. "At least Dr. Moser had the decency to commit suicide and save his family embarrassment."

Megan and I were nearly home when I thought of a question. "Why didn't you call Jerry once you knew Dr. Moser was guilty? Why did you take such a risk as to confront the good doctor yourself?"

"Because Jerry would have arrested Dr. Moser."

"Of course. Dr. Moser was a murderer."

"Sometimes justice is found outside the courtroom."

I stopped the truck in my driveway and turned to look at her. "Did you know Moser would kill himself?"

She never answered me—then, or in all the time since.

SELECTED BIBLIOGRAPHY OF STRING-FIGURE BOOKS AND ARTICLES

ELFFERS, JOOST AND MICHAEL SCHUYT, *Cat's Cradles and Other String Figures.* New York: Penguin Books, 1979.

GRYSKI, CAMILLA, *Cat's Cradle, Owl's Eyes: A Book of String Games.* New York: William Morrow and Co., 1983.
———, *Many Stars & More String Games.* New York: William Morrow and Co., 1985.
———, *Super String Games.* New York: William Morrow and Co., 1987.
Bulletin of the International String Figure Association. Pasadena, CA: ISFA Press. Volume 3, 1996.
Bulletin of the International String Figure Association. Pasadena, CA: ISFA Press, Vol. 4, 1997.
"The Moon Gone Dark." *String Figure Magazine,* Volume 1, Number 4 (December 1996).

JAYNE, CAROLINE F., *String Figures and How to Make Them.* Reprint, New York: Dover Publications, 1962.